Spell Disaster

Silver Hollow
Paranormal Cozy Mystery Book 2

Leighann Dobbs
Traci Douglass

This is a work of fiction.

None of it is real. All names, places, and events are products of the author's imagination. Any resemblance to real names, places, or events are purely coincidental, and should not be construed as being real.

Chapter One

"What do you think?" Issy Quinn asked Brimstone, a large, pudgy-faced gray cat with hellfire orange eyes and an attitude to match. "Life is idyllic with Enchanted Pets."

"I think you best get a shovel, because it's piling up pretty high in here," the cat said, jumping up onto the top shelf against the wall and settling in for a nice long nap. "You can do better."

"Not helpful." Issy sighed. She'd been working on a new catchphrase for her magical pet store all morning and wasn't making much headway. Of course, the fact that she'd just received a new shipment of guests this morning didn't help matters. At least her new batch of familiars seemed to be adjusting well to life in the small New Hampshire town of Silver Hollow. Some of them would start assisting their owners soon, and some—like Gordon—would get a very special home. She glanced over into his tropically bedecked vivarium and saw the cute little bearded dragon perched between two palm fronds. One of his front feet was raised in her direction, as if he were waving.

Issy waved back and grinned. Wouldn't do to offend the special little lizard. Her instincts told her Gordon would belong to someone very important. Maybe a high-level witch or warlock. Who exactly, she wasn't sure yet. But the right familiar always found their person.

Smiling, she turned back to Brimstone. "So, give me some suggestions, please."

"How about you relax and close early today?" The feline stretched lazily then squinted at her, his eyes mere slits. "You should enjoy the blissful quiet after all the disruption of the murder and that hateful dark pagan, Christian. I, for one, am completely taxed and need to catch up on my nap time."

"Well, I can't close early." Issy tossed aside her notebook and pen then stared out the store's front windows and down the street into the nearly deserted town green. "Some of us have a business to run."

"Business looks flat to me." Brimstone yawned then flopped onto his side, down for the count.

Issy shook her head and sighed. Oh, to be a cat. Then she glanced at the green once more. Over the past month, the Silver Hollow Visitors'

Board had placed several new wrought-iron benches around the perimeter of the green and spiffed up the landscaping, all in hopes of bringing in more tourists and their money to the area.

On one of those benches sat her latest problem, Luigi Romano. He'd been sent by the committee—a universal entity that presided over witchcraft and other magic—to keep tabs on the local paranormal population after the whole Louella Drummond debacle. The man seemed nice enough, but Issy still couldn't wait for him to leave. Weird how he always wore that black duster coat, even in the dead heat of summer. And that beard, all bushy and brown to match his wild long hair and the gazillion earrings glinting from his ears. If she didn't know better, she'd say he looked as though he belonged more on the set of some sci-fi western movie than in their small, quiet New England village.

She turned back to the counter and cursed under her breath. "Oh, newt shizzle."

Brimstone peeked open one eye. "Problem?"

"Yes. As a matter of fact. I need to do something to drum up business, but I can't think up a decent catchphrase for the store with that spy sitting out there watching every move I make. It's enough to make a witch go batty."

Near her feet, Issy's adorable Pomeranian familiar—Bella—yipped, as if in agreement. Issy focused on the pup, a feeling of warmth spreading in her chest. She'd been without a familiar for a long time and had wondered if she'd ever find one to bond with. One look at Bella with her thick orange fur and soulful brown eyes, and she'd been smitten. Now, if only she could start to communicate with her... well, no sense in rushing things. Creating the witch-familiar bond took time.

She stared at the dog, looking for some sort of telepathic communication. For a second, she thought she sensed something. A slight vibration, and the thought "tall, dark, and handsome" appeared in her head. A feeling of satisfaction flared, then worry. She sure hoped Bella wasn't communicating about Luigi. Tall and dark. Yes. Handsome? Nope.

"Well, given the complete lack of any excitement around town these days, I'm sure Luigi will be gone soon." Brimstone yawned then rolled over to face away from Issy. "Stop worrying so much. It only makes for bad energy."

Resigned, Issy picked up Bella and walked over to the windows. Maybe Bella's assessment of Luigi was a little off, but she was still in training. Bella's skills were strengthening more each day. She didn't doubt for a second that the tiny puffball was trying to tell her something. "That's my beautiful girl," she crooned, kissing the dog's head repeatedly. "Who's a good familiar, huh? Who's the best little familiar ever?"

"Hello?" Brimstone languidly raised his paw. "That would be me."

"You're too independent to be considered a mere familiar, and besides, you have ages of experience," Issy said. "Bella's just now coming into her own."

"I'll alert the press." Brimstone's tone sounded completely unimpressed. Then again, given the cat's age and intelligence, it wasn't surprising. He really was the best familiar Issy had ever encountered, even if he did have an independent streak that made it seem more as though he were the boss and she were here to do *his* bidding. Either way, she wouldn't tell Brimstone that anytime soon. His ego barely fit through the door as it was.

Through the windows, she spotted the jack-in-the-pulpits her cousin and local magical landscaper extraordinaire, Raine, had planted a few weeks back. The plants were in full bloom now, their hooded flowers reminding her of the specks of green in Dex's hazel eyes. Her heart pinched, and she squeezed her eyes shut at the memories.

Dex Nolan was an investigator for the Federal Bureau of Paranormal Investigations, otherwise known as the FBPI. The FBPI was a secret government entity—a branch of the FBI—chartered to investigate paranormals. And not in a good way. In a dissecting, torturing, and brain-picking way. Rumor had it that they had a laboratory in the Mojave Desert called Area 59, where they performed all kinds of unthinkable experiments trying to figure out what made paranormals tick. For decades, Silver Hollow had escaped their scrutiny, but a certain incident a few months back with a dark witch had brought the town in general, and Issy in particular, into their crosshairs.

Dex Nolan hadn't seemed like the kind of guy who wished harm on paranormals. He and Issy had gotten to know each other a bit during the Drummond murder case. Yes, she'd kissed him in the woods, and sure, it had been pretty fantastic, but he was gone now, back to FBPI headquarters, and wouldn't be returning. At least she hoped not, anyway. No matter how attractive she found him, the last thing she needed was him nosing around again.

9

Having hulking Luigi shadowing her every move was bad enough.

Located on the opposite side of the street from Enchanted Pets was Sheer Magic, the beauty salon owned by her other cousin, Gray. He had a knack for making all the local ladies lovely. Women left his shop with haircuts that complemented the shape of their face perfectly. And their hair color was phenomenal. It was said that one of his cuts could make you look ten years younger. His shop was constantly busy, and today appeared to be no exception, with patrons filling the chairs inside and all of his cutting stations full.

"They're assigning someone you know. The FBPI." Brimstone said, his sleepy voice a rough purr. "To live in Silver Hollow."

Issy didn't need to ask why he had suddenly blurted that out. She knew better than to leave her thoughts unguarded around the powerful feline, but today she was distracted, and he'd sensed her thoughts about Dex. "Raine said something about how the FBPI sent agents to infiltrate paranormal communities, but..."

Her words trailed off as she spied Enid Pettywood leaving Sheer Magic. The older lady tottered outside with the help of her cane, still wearing a set of high-heeled pumps that would've given Issy second thoughts. Most women she knew of a certain age gave up the glam shoes in favor of something more comfortable. But not Enid. She had to love the older lady for that, along with so many other things too.

Enid walked to the curb and gazed around, looking as cute as a button in her new curly style, courtesy of Gray. Beside her, on a purple leash, was her potbellied pig familiar, Becky.

A few moments later, Enid's granddaughter, Nikki, joined the elderly woman on the sidewalk. From the way Nikki looked put together for once, Issy guessed she'd gotten a fresh haircut too. The younger woman's steps faltered as well, but not from old age.

Word around Silver Hollow said Nikki liked to drink. A lot. Still, the girl made time to have tea with Enid every afternoon, and that counted for something in Issy's book, even if the drinking made Nikki a bit unstable. Not an ideal situation, but poor Enid didn't have any other family around to help. The Quinn cousins also tried to keep an eye on the older witch when they could, but making sure Enid stayed out of trouble sometimes seemed like a full-time occupation. The elderly woman's spells had a way of going askew...

Issy watched as the two women said their good-byes then parted ways. Enid started across the street toward the green while Nikki walked a few doors down to enter O'Hara's Pub. Enid moved at a pretty good clip too, despite the cane and her age. In fact, Issy would describe the pep in her step as downright spry today.

Raine and Issy's other cousin, Ember—a magical chocolatier—reported seeing Enid pretty regularly these days at the town's newest hot spot, The Main Squeeze. Catering to the world's recent health kick, the place was an all-natural juice bar, claiming to "heal what ails you."

Issy snorted. Now that was a good catchphrase. Maybe she should hire Karen Dixon, the juice bar owner, to help her with her store's tagline.

"Time to get back to work." Turning away from the windows, Issy kissed Bella's head once more before putting her down then headed back over to brainstorm again on her slogan. She'd just started getting into a creative groove when Bella's sharp yip snagged her attention.

"What is it, girl?" Issy moved toward the windows once more and crouched next to her tiny Pom, who was staring outside. "What's going on?"

Bella raised a front paw and pointed outside. Issy gasped as she spotted Enid in the alleyway between the hair salon and the neighboring building, lurching precariously, one of her high heels apparently stuck in a crack.

Without a second thought, Issy rushed out of Enchanted Pets and sprinted across the green toward Enid. The elderly witch could fall and break a hip or worse. It would only take one car, one unobservant driver, to hit the poor old lady and take her out.

As she reached the other side of the block, Issy glanced into Sheer Magic and caught Gray's eye. If Enid was really wedged in tight, she'd need some extra muscle to help her out. Her cousin rushed out of his salon and met her at the curb. Together, they jogged over to where Enid floundered, her arms pinwheeling. Becky stood to her side, making little pig snorts of distress.

"Oh dear," Enid said as they arrived. "I'll just cast a release spell here and—"

"No, no. Wait!" Issy tried to calm the older woman before she did something drastic. The last spell Enid had attempted had gone horribly awry, resulting in one of Issy's frogs being transformed into a flowering quince. Enid had been going for a Prince Charming, but her pronunciation had gotten bungled and...

"A little help here," Gray said, trying to get ahold of Enid's magic cane. She used it like a wand to cast her wonky spells. "Enid, honey. Just give me the cane."

"Oh, my cane!" Enid said. "Thank you for reminding me, Graeme."

Only Enid called Gray by his full name.

Before Issy or Gray could take the thing away, Enid brandished it before her and muttered an incantation:

"Bealzabob bealzebeman.

Release my heel, and let me free, man."

A large poof sounded, and the air filled with gray smoke and the smell of sulphur. Lost in the fog, Issy squinted over at Gray in time to see a giant black hole open up near Enid—gaping and bottomless. Both Quinn cousins reached for Enid to save her, but another poof sounded, this time accompanied by a whoosh of hot air. The black hole vanished, leaving Enid free and stumbling to the side.

"What the heck was that?" Gray asked, coughing.

"No idea." Issy clutched the obsidian talisman in her pocket tighter. It was supposed to ward off any evil, and after what they'd just witnessed, it seemed they could use all the help they could get right about now. She gently took

Enid's arm with her free hand and guided the older woman safely back up onto the sidewalk. "Are you all right, Enid?"

"Why yes, dear. I'm fine. How are you?"

Issy opened her mouth to answer then snapped it shut as Luigi rounded the corner, a pizza box in his hand. He stopped near Gray's side and looked the buff hairdresser up and down. "What's going on here?"

"Nothing," Gray said, his gaze darting to Issy. "What's happening with you?"

Luigi sniffed the air, his nose wrinkled. "What's that smell? Sulphur? Are you performing illegal acts of magic here?"

"No, no." Issy moved closer to Enid's side and pointed at the small potbellied pig with a fake laugh. "That was Becky. She had gas. Boy, those pigs smell awful, don't they?" She elbowed Enid in the side. "Don't they, Enid?"

"Ow, dear. You really shouldn't—"

At Issy's pointed stare, the older woman's eyes widened, and she nodded slowly, comprehension dawning in her gaze.

"Oh, right, right, dear." Enid smiled. "Yes, these pigs smell terrible sometimes. Why, I remember a time when I fed little Becky here too much rhubarb, and oh, man. I almost had to purchase a gas mask. And don't even get me started on the fruits and leafy greens, really. One time—"

"That's great, Enid." Gray put his muscled arm around her shoulders. "I'm sure Luigi here gets the idea."

"Yeah," Luigi said, his expression skeptical. "I get the picture, all right."

Enid eyed the pizza box in the man's hand. "Did you know I have a famous secret pizza sauce recipe, Mr. Romano? I didn't realize I'd be running into you today, but I promise to get back to you with it, if you'd like. Now come along, Becky." She tottered off once more, her tiny pig in tow.

"Secret recipe, huh?" Luigi said. All three of them watched the elderly lady go. "I might take her up on that."

Issy grasped the opportunity with both hands. "Do you like to cook, Luigi?"

"Sometimes." He eyed her suspiciously. "Might even open my own restaurant around here. Show you all what the best pizza in the area tastes like."

"Best pizza?" Gray took Issy's hand and tugged her toward the front door of Sheer Magic. "That sounds amazing. Must get back to work now. See you later!"

Gray waved then pulled Issy inside his shop and through the crowded waiting room to the empty supply area in the back of the store. "What happened out there?"

"I don't know." Issy frowned. "Enid's spells rarely work correctly, and that whole sulphur cloud and black hole..." She shuddered. "I've got a bad feeling about this."

"Yeah, me too. I know she meant to say 'free, man,' but what if it came out as something else? You know how her spells often screw up in rhyme. What if she summoned a demon?"

"We better hope that's not what happened. If so, we'll never get rid of Luigi." Pulse thudding loud in her ears, Issy exhaled. "It's bad enough he scrutinizes every act of magic to make sure it's on the up and up. If he thinks there's demon activity involved too, he'll be on the warpath to find the culprit."

"Not to mention poor old Enid would never survive the punishment."

"We can't just let this go. We need to find out for sure if there is a demon and what it's up to. We'll need to convene our cousin coven. Tonight work for you?"

"I'll be there after I close the shop at seven," Gray said. "Your place?"

"Yep." Issy waved and headed back to Enchanted Pets.

Chapter Two

Issy had a small cottage on the shore of Solstice Lake. It wasn't big, and it wasn't fancy, but it had its own stretch of beach, and the view of the mountains behind the lake framed by tall Scotch pines was priceless.

The cousins often convened here around Issy's stone fire pit when they had important things to discuss. And tonight they had something very important to discuss.

It was summer, and the sun was still up at 7:00 p.m., though it was low in the sky, painting the undersides of the fluffy white clouds a pale pink that was reflected in the sky-blue waters. At this time of night, the lake surface was as calm as a mirror. The low chirping of crickets and the scent of pine trees mixed with campfire created a serene atmosphere. But that outward serenity was a stark contrast to the nervousness that thrummed inside Issy as she waited for her cousins to arrive.

Ember was the first, carrying her kittens, Bellatrix and Endora, in a cauldron-shaped tote bag, as they were still too young to trot around on their own.

"How is the bonding coming?" Issy asked as Ember took out first Bellatrix, the white one, and then Endora, the black one, and set them on the ground. As soon as they were loose, Bella ran over, and the three of them sniffed each other in greeting then tumbled happily in a ball of black, white, and orange fur.

"Pretty good. I think Endora tried to communicate a thought to me today." Ember smiled fondly at the cats and then turned to Issy. "What about you?"

"Bella is coming along. She might have tried to tell me something about Luigi this morning, but it was a bit garbled," Issy said.

"Well, it does take months and sometimes even years for the bonding to happen."

"I know. Though having Brimstone around might not be helping. He can be kind of a negative influence, and I hope his vibes aren't stunting Bella's growth."

Raine came around the side of the house, holding her familiar, Mortimer, a Venus flytrap, in her arms. "Brimstone talks tough, but he's very fond of the new familiars. They'll come along in time. Just like Morty." Raine tapped the plant pot affectionately.

"What's it like communicating with a plant?" Issy asked. Raine's way with plants was legendary, so it wasn't unusual that her familiar was a Venus flytrap. But Issy had never been able to communicate with plants. Dogs, cats, even lizards and toads, yes, but not plants. "Do they have the same kinds of thoughts as animals?"

Raine shrugged and poked a stick into the fire pit, sending orange sparks up into the air. "Sort of, you just have to know how to interpret them. Plants are better at some things than animals. And it's much easier to leave them somewhere and have them absorb the feelings and emotions. Remember how we did that at Hans Geller's?"

Raine referred to earlier in the summer when they'd been tracking down a dark witch. They'd left Mortimer in an office where they thought there might be nefarious dealings. In that way, a plant was much superior as a familiar because you could plunk them anywhere and no one would think twice. That came in handy since Issy or Ember couldn't very well leave the kittens or Bella at someone's office. "I suppose Morty does have his uses."

"And he looks good on an end table," Ember added.

They all sat down around the fire pit and grabbed the sticks they'd whittled down to perfect marshmallow-roasting points. Issy stretched her feet out, digging her toes into the warm sand.

"You really think Enid conjured a demon?" Raine asked, her face illuminated by the huge campfire. "Issy, can you pass the marshmallows?"

"Sure thing." She picked up the bag and passed them to Ember, who sat beside her around the large fire pit. "And yeah, I'm pretty sure. That black hole was not normal." Issy shivered despite the heat of the flames and the warm summer night. "You guys should've seen it —all big and dark and fathomless."

"Yikes." Ember took out a marshmallow and jabbed it onto the end of her stick before handing the bag to Raine. Her long wavy hair looked even darker auburn tonight, and her emerald eyes sparkled. "That sounds terrifying."

"Terrifying and stinky," Gray said, joining their group, his large white cockatoo familiar, Cosmo, perched on his shoulder. "Sorry I'm late. Got behind with a cut and style."

"No problem." Raine handed him a roasting stick. "S'mores again. Courtesy of Issy and Ember."

"Awesome." Gray took a seat on a log beside Issy then picked up one of the homemade chocolate bars and narrowed his aqua eyes on Ember. "These aren't enchanted, are they? I've got enough trouble keeping the ladies at bay."

"Not a drop of love potion. Witch's honor." Ember crossed her heart and grinned. "I can't help it, though, if you're just a born stud muffin."

Gray shook his head and stared into the fire. With his muscled brawn and shoulder-length midnight-black hair, he looked as though he'd walked right off the decks of some pirate ship. The bird only added to his swashbuckling aura.

Issy chuckled. "Hard day at the office?"

"You have no idea." He sighed. "My power went out three times this afternoon."

"Mine too," Issy said. "Another reason why I'm afraid Enid might have summoned a demon. I seem to recall something about them messing around with energy."

"Could be." Raine stroked Morty's leaves. "I've heard that too."

"What do you think it wants?" Ember nibbled on a freshly made s'more and cuddled Endora and Bellatrix, in her lap.

"Don't know." Issy poked her empty stick into the fire, stirring the coals. Bella snoozed on the ground near her feet. "We're not even sure what kind it is yet. Or even if there *is* one."

"The power outages could be everyone's air conditioners. It's been sweltering, and demand might overload the system." Gray stopped with his s'more halfway to his mouth as all attention zeroed in on him. His cockatoo familiar, Cosmo, squawked loudly from his left shoulder. "Or not."

"At least that excuse will give us a good cover with the normal folk around town," Issy offered. "And, hopefully, Luigi."

"Ugh. Seriously, people." Brimstone strutted over and took residence on the log beside Ember. He eyed the young kittens warily then preened a moment before continuing. "It doesn't matter what kind of demon it is. They all wreak havoc by attaching to energy because they have no physical body. Everyone knows this."

Issy stuck a marshmallow onto her stick then plunged it into the fire once more. "Okay, say we're dealing with a phantom demon who craves voltage. Where will he get it?"

"Wherever he can," Brimstone continued. "Computers. Light fixtures. Car batteries. Anywhere with a power source."

"Huh." Raine shoved her last bite of graham cracker into her mouth, her stick-straight copper hair brushing her shoulders as she shrugged.

"Well, I guess we can count ourselves lucky it's not like the demons in all those horror movies. They like to possess people's bodies and make them do heinous things."

Brimstone narrowed his orange gaze but remained silent.

"Okay." Issy blew on her toasted marshmallow, then slid it off between two chocolate-bar-lined graham crackers and squished it all together before taking a bite. The sweetness of the crackers and smoky melted marshmallow blended perfectly with the slight bitterness of the chocolate and tasted like nirvana. "These are yummy by the way, Ember."

"Mmm." Gray agreed around a mouthful of food. Once he swallowed, he said, "So what do we do now? Power outages, fathomless holes, the stinky smell of sulphur—seems like Enid really might have summoned a demon. Maybe it's all a big coincidence, but we can't take that chance with Luigi breathing down our necks. He's already suspicious. So, say Enid did summon a demon, how would we get rid of it?"

"Sage," Ember said, her tone decisive. "It's the ultimate purifier. Demons hate sage. All we have to do is burn some and send the thing back to where it came from."

"Finding it shouldn't be hard, right?" Raine stood and wiped her hands down the front of her overalls. Given that she spent most of her days digging in the dirt or holed away in her greenhouse, her practical outfit made sense. "All we have to do is follow these weird electrical outages. If there's a demon, we'll send it back, and if not, then no harm done."

"Sounds good to me. I say we get on it." Gray pushed to his feet as well then ran his finger down Cosmo's back. "The sooner, the better. Before anything worse happens."

"Agreed." Ember placed her kittens back into the tote bag beside her.

"I've got sage handy already. Just let me know where and when." Raine hefted Morty's pot onto her hip.

"Cool." Issy picked up a tired Bella. "I'll see if I can figure out a pattern to the energy fluctuations. Maybe we can use them to predict where this demon might strike next. If so, there's a chance we can get there first and banish it once and for all, before Luigi even suspects it's here."

Chapter Three

The next afternoon, Issy sat beneath a dryer at Sheer Magic, listening intently to the conversations around her. Everyone knew that the best place to find out all the local gossip was on Tuesday afternoons at her cousin's hair salon, so after lunch, she'd left Enchanted Pets in the hands of her trusty assistant, Hannah, and headed on over. Besides, she'd been overdue for a cut, anyway.

The cashier at the local pharmacy sat to her right and chatted away endlessly on her phone about their weird power outage earlier that morning around six. Issy scribbled the time and location down in her notebook then tuned into the conversation to her left—the wife of Silver Hollow's grocery store owner. According to that lady, all their freezers had died about three hours after the pharmacy outage. Behind her, the gal who ran the register at the penny candy store said they had a blackout three hours after that.

Pattern detected.

It seemed that their demon needed an energy feed every three hours.

Issy then sketched out a crude map of Silver Hollow. By connecting the dots of the three locations, it gave her a rough idea of the direction the demon was moving in. If her hunches were correct, that meant the demon should make his next move on the town's diner at...

She glanced at her watch.

Three p.m.

Adrenaline coursing through her bloodstream, Issy pulled out her phone to text Raine and Ember then slid out from beneath her dryer and headed to where Gray was working his magic on one of his patrons.

"I've got the next location," she whispered while her cousin snipped tiny sections of hair. "Three o'clock this afternoon. The diner on the corner. You in?"

"Aw, I can't today. Playing catch-up after yesterday's outages. I'll send you good vibes, though."

"Okay." Issy removed the salon's black smock then finger-styled her strawberry-blond curls in the mirror before heading out. "See you around."

"See you," Gray called from behind her. "Be careful. And stay out of trouble."

Two hours later, the three female Quinn cousins sat on a bench in the town green, staring at the tiny diner on the corner. Through the restaurant's front windows, Issy spotted Enid inside, and her heart ached a bit for the elderly woman eating all alone. It was better she didn't know about the demon she may have conjured. With her memory issues and all, Enid had enough problems. Besides, Issy and her cousins could handle the demon on their own.

"Did you bring the good sage?" Issy asked Raine.

"Heck yeah." She held up a black-ribbon-tied bundle. "Most potent in the bunch and straight from my greenhouse."

"Great." After a quick check of her watch, Issy stood and started toward the alleyway beside the diner. "Let's go."

They crossed the street. Enid saw them through the window and waved. Rushing, the three hurried past the diner and into the mouth of the alley, taking refuge against a tall fence that encircled the restaurant's dumpster.

Raine wrinkled her nose at the smelly scent of rot in the air. "Remind me again why we can't do this inside?"

"Why don't you just send Luigi Romano an engraved invitation to come arrest you too while you're at it?" Issy gave her cousin a perturbed look. "We can't just walk in there and start burning sage and exorcising demons."

"Point taken," Raine said. "Luigi's presence is an added complication to this whole mix. Do you really think he would throw the book at Enid?"

"I was wondering that too," Ember said. "He doesn't seem as mean or tough as I thought he'd be. I would have thought the committee would be ready to crack down after they caught someone in Silver Hollow doing dark magic. But Luigi seems kind of mellow."

"He didn't seem mellow when he thought Enid or Gray or I were practicing illegal magic yesterday." Issy chewed on her bottom lip. "But now that you mention it, he isn't as mean as I expected him to be. And all this business with the pizza. He seems to be more focused on that than on finding violations for the committee."

"Maybe he has another agenda," Raine suggested.

"Maybe, but right now, we need to get rid of this demon whether Luigi is going to punish Enid or not. It won't do to have a demon loose in town."

"No kidding." Ember made a face. "I ruined two batches of fudge this morning because the electricity went out."

"We can't have that," Raine said. "Could start a riot in town."

Issy shushed them both. "Keep your voices down. We don't want anyone coming back here and sticking their noses into our little exorcism." She pointed toward the brick wall. "The diner's electrical box is right there. If our demon starts blowing circuits, we'll know he's fighting us. If not, I think we can assume we've vanquished him."

"Fine," Raine whispered. "Let's just hurry, okay? Before I pass out from the stench." She carefully snipped off a large stem of sage and whispered an incantation before setting it ablaze then walked around in a small circle, eyes closed, repeating the same spell seven times. Finally, she stopped and opened her eyes, smiling. "Done."

"All righty, then." Ember sighed. "Seems to have worked. No power zaps to report so far."

"Yep." Issy checked her watch again. 3:05. It seemed that they had done it. She gave a relieved sigh and rolled her tense shoulders. "Well, that was ea—"

A bloodcurdling scream pierced the air, and Issy's stomach lurched.

All three cousins slowly peeked around the edge of the fence to see a terrifying sight.

The cook from the diner stood over the dead body of a young redheaded dishwasher. A meat cleaver protruded ominously from the victim's back while blood pooled on the trash below her. The distinct smell of sulphur wafted through the scene.

It seemed that the demon had struck again.

And, this time, it had turned deadly.

Chapter Four

"Explain to me again what you guys are doing here," Deputy Deirdre Clawson—otherwise known as DeeDee—of the Silver Hollow PD said. She eyed the three Quinn cousins pointedly while the town sheriff, Owen Gleason, processed the murder scene.

"We were just out for a walk," Issy said. "Don't tell me that's against the law now too."

"No. Walking's fine." DeeDee glanced behind her then leaned closer. EMTs zipped the victim into a body bag then wheeled the gurney over to the waiting ambulance that would take the body to the hospital morgue. "As long as that's all you were doing."

DeeDee, being a werewolf shifter and part of the paranormal community of Silver Hollow, served as more than an upholder of the law in town. She kept their all-too-human sheriff from finding out about all the magic lurking just beneath their tiny lakeside village's surface.

"Of course that's all we were doing," Ember said. "Why would you think otherwise?"

"Well, let's see. Maybe because of all the stuff that went down with the Drummond case? Or maybe because mayhem follows you Quinns around like a loyal pup? Or maybe..." DeeDee raised her superhumanly sensitive nose and sniffed. "Because it smells an awful lot like sage out here."

Raine harrumphed and crossed her arms. "We were just standing there, behind the fence, when we heard the scream. Witch's honor."

"For all your sakes, I hope that's true." DeeDee turned back to watch Owen dig around in the dumpster for any clues they might've missed, and Issy couldn't help noticing her spiffy new uniform. It looked several sizes smaller than before, and her hair and makeup were done too. Huh. It seemed that ever since Gray had done a full-moon ritual on DeeDee's behalf earlier in the summer, she was turning into quite a fashion plate. She'd even gotten a new hairstyle from him.

Issy didn't blame her, though. DeeDee hadn't been blessed with sleek good looks. She'd been a bit on the feral side and downright hairy before. But Gray's ritual had spiffed her up. And she was definitely taking advantage of her new good looks with the eligible bachelors in town. Issy didn't blame her on that either. According to wolf pack rules, DeeDee might not have long to sow her wild oats.

The deputy glanced back at Issy, gaze narrowed. "Are there any *peculiar* elements I should keep away from Owen?"

"Honestly, I'm not sure." Issy stopped short of mentioning the demon they'd been tracking. She didn't like keeping things from DeeDee, but for all she knew, this really could've been just a regular old murder. Never mind the lingering bubble of dread swelling in her chest that told her otherwise.

Taking Raine by the arm, Issy drew her cousin away from the others a few steps. "Are you sure that sage was strong enough?"

"Define sure," Raine said.

Ember joined them, frowning. "She grows the most potent sage in three counties. If that's not enough to banish bad demons, I don't know what is."

"DeeDee, I need an evidence container," Owen called from where he was crouched beside the dumpster, his right arm halfway under it.

"Oh, newt shizzle. That doesn't sound good." Issy exhaled slowly then moved closer to the crime scene again to see what they'd found. She'd never seen Owen process a crime scene so diligently before. Then again, they didn't usually have murders in the Hollow. Not until recently, anyway, and ever since the last murder, Owen had been getting more serious about his job. Issy wasn't convinced that was a good thing.

Owen was a good guy, but she preferred it when he made surfing and paddleboarding a priority. It was better for the paranormals if he didn't pay much attention to the crimes in town. Owen knew nothing of paranormal activity, and they'd learned long ago, the less the humans were exposed to the magic side of things, the better. Not only that, but when a paranormal crime ended in a murder investigation, things could get sticky.

Owen pulled what looked like a crudely made doll out from under the dumpster. Its arms were twigs and the body made from straw. Nose scrunched, he held it between his gloved fingers before plopping it into the evidence bag DeeDee held open for him. "No idea what that thing is, but it looks an awful lot like our victim. Same hair on top and everything."

"A voodoo doll," Raine whispered.

"Yep." Issy swallowed hard. "Which means the killer picked out the victim beforehand."

"This is good. Means we've got ourselves evidence of premeditation," Owen said.

DeeDee held up the bag and squinted. "Only one problem, boss."

"What's that?" Owen asked as he headed for the back of the ambulance.

"This doll has a blue noose tied around its neck, suggesting hanging or strangulation. Our victim was stabbed," DeeDee called.

"Good point. Maybe the killer tried to strangle the victim and it didn't work, then had to resort to the cleaver." Owen climbed into the rig and unzipped the body bag then peered inside at the corpse. Issy and her cousins followed DeeDee to back of the ambulance. "Darn. No marks on the victim's neck that I can see." He peeked farther under the body bag then scowled. "What's this?"

"What, boss?" DeeDee asked, giving Issy a concerned look.

"This." Owen held up one of the victim's arms and pointed at her inner wrist.

There, burned into the flesh, was a small black spiral surrounded by spikes.

The mark of a demon kill.

"Oh, uh, uh... *that*." DeeDee's stammer, coupled with her fear-filled eyes, had Issy's dread boiling over into full-blown panic. It seemed that their demon had graduated from draining appliances and power blackouts to murder.

The deputy tried to play it off as best she could, though her wide-eyed stare remained on Issy the whole time. "Some tattoo, huh, boss? Saw that same design on one of the tourists last week. Some shop over in Bristol does them. I'll check it out later and see if they remember our victim, if you want, Owen."

"Right." Issy backed away slowly, taking her cousins with her. "We'll just be going, then, too, if you don't need anything else from us."

"What I need is for you guys to figure out what the heck is happening here," DeeDee said as she caught up with them, her voice still holding an edge of fear. "If there's a rogue demon on the loose, we need to stop it. Fast. I'll do my best to keep this all hidden from Owen for as long as I can, but you need to be quick."

"Sure. Thanks, DeeDee." Issy stumbled away, feeling drained. "We'll let you know as soon as we find something."

"Whoa. This is bad," Ember said once they'd reached the main street again. The sun still shined brightly, at direct odds with the gruesome scene back in that alleyway. "This is really, really bad."

"Who would do something like that?" Raine shook her head, her expression mortified. "That's beyond dark magic. Not to mention the bad karma associated with taking a life."

"I don't know." Issy held onto to her cousins as they crossed the street then flopped down on a deserted bench, craving the safety of contact. "I don't think a regular paranormal could allow themselves to be possessed on their own. Which means whoever is responsible must've been weak or wounded, or in some way susceptible to dark forces."

"I did some research last night. Demons can hop right into physical bodies if they find an entry point. A wound or some kind of illness that makes a person weak and susceptible," Raine added.

"How can we possibly find that out, though?" Ember sighed. "It's not like paranormals broadcast their weaknesses to the world. This is going to be a lot of work."

"Yep." Raine's shoulders slumped. "But what choice do we have?"

"We don't. And we don't have much time either." Issy glanced over her shoulder and spotted Luigi Romano heading toward the commotion in the alley. Exactly what she didn't need right now. "Like DeeDee said, we need to find out who did this and banish that demon before something worse happens."

Chapter Five

"I can't believe someone would kill the dishwasher from the diner. And she was just a young girl, not more than twenty. She came in to get her hair cut once," Gray said. All four Quinn cousins were sitting back around Issy's fire pit overlooking the lake. "It's so wrong."

"Believe it," Issy said, squeezing her eyes shut against the awful images flooding back into her mind. "And that *someone* is possessed by a demon."

"But why would the demon want to kill a dishwasher?" Gray asked again.

"Had nothing to do with her occupation." Raine passed around a plate of veggies and dip. "This probably means we've got a demon who's looking for a permanent human host. And it wouldn't care what she did for a job."

"Why do you say that?" Ember asked, filling up her plate with carrots and celery.

"I've researched these things. Remember that online course I took last year for my Herbal Sorceress certification?" Raine nibbled on a broccoli floret. "There was a whole lesson on creating potions and tinctures to combat possessions. I didn't think of it earlier as our demon seemed content to mess around with light fixtures and freezers. I didn't realize it was going to actually possess a human."

"That means you're an expert?" Issy asked, her tone hopeful.

"Unfortunately, no. I was out that week because of the annual Harvest Moon festival." Raine shrugged one shoulder. "I vaguely remember something about them having to kill a certain number of people. You know, trade their souls in before they get to take up permanent residence in a body. I've still got the class materials somewhere. I'll see if I can find them."

"Good luck." Issy smiled. The messiness of Raine's office was legendary. The chances of her finding anything in there seemed slim to none. "There's a new moon in five days. This demon might try to harness that power to stay on earth. Maybe there's some other rituals or criteria they have to fulfill in order to escape Hades and inhabit the earthly realm."

"If that last part's true, then we probably haven't seen the last death in Silver Hollow." Gray took the platter Issy handed him and piled a paper plate high with veggies and dip. Cosmo squawked from his perch on the end of the log, and Gray tossed him a slice of cucumber to keep him quiet. "What about the police?"

"DeeDee said she'd keep Owen off track for as long as she could." Issy pushed a pebble around with the toe of her boot while absently stroking Bella's silky fur. She'd waited all day for some sort of communication from the little pup but got nothing. Now Bella was worn out from playing with Bellatrix and Endora, who slept wrapped around the base of Mortimer's pot near Raine's feet. The only familiar missing was Brimstone, though that wasn't unusual. He came and went as he pleased.

"Not sure how long DeeDee will be able to keep Owen off track after he found that voodoo doll," Ember said. "He seemed pretty excited about it."

"Yeah, and we never got a chance to tell her how Enid summoned the demon. Though she saw the demon-kill mark on the victim's wrist, and I bet she's dying to find out more. Didn't want to talk about it too much with all the people milling about behind the restaurant," Raine added.

As if on cue, the sound of tires crunching on Issy's gravel driveway sounded, followed by the cutting of an engine and the pounding of footsteps. Soon, DeeDee stuck her head around the corner of the house. "Hey Quinns. Hope it's okay I dropped by."

"Sure. We were kind of expecting you." Issy waved her over. "What's going on, Deputy? Have a seat, and help yourself to some veggies."

DeeDee took a seat on the opposite end of Gray's log and grabbed a plate. "Well, I'm afraid I've got some bad news on the Owen front."

"Uh-oh," Ember said. "What?"

"He's all excited about the case." DeeDee took a bite of cauliflower with dip before continuing. "This is really good, Raine. These from your gardens?"

"Of course." Raine grinned. "Why is Owen excited?"

"Oh." DeeDee wiped her mouth with a napkin. "He thinks he'll finally have a chance to prove his detective skills by solving the case. He's been taking his police duties a lot more seriously lately."

"Yeah, that's not good," Gray said.

"Means I'll have to work harder." DeeDee crunched down on a carrot. "Would help if I knew what was *really* going on."

"We think Enid Pettywood may have inadvertently summoned a demon outside of Sheer Magic this morning."

"What?" DeeDee set her half-finished plate aside. "How?"

"She got her foot caught in a crack in the street and tried to cast a spell to free herself," Gray said. "You know how she gets flustered, though, and doesn't always enunciate well."

"Yeah." Issy shrugged. "Plus, it would explain all the power disturbances around town."

"Is that what happened?" DeeDee leaned forward. "Ours blipped out at the station too. Thank goodness we had a generator to keep us going."

"We're pretty sure the power outages are demon related. The murder too." Issy picked up Bella, who whined in her sleep, and cradled the tiny dog in her arms. "So, as you can see, we have two problems. One is that there is a demon loose, killing people, and the other is that Owen might erroneously arrest the human body that did the killing."

"Yep, big problems. I thought that was a demon-kill mark on the body. I sent Owen to a couple of tattoo parlors to check it out. Implied maybe the dishwasher associated with an unsavory crowed. Figured that might keep him busy going down dead ends for a while. But it's going to be difficult to divert his attention and keep him otherwise occupied."

"I know, but we can't let him arrest whoever's body the demon is possessing. It wouldn't be right," Raine said.

"And you know how demons are, as soon as the body was incarcerated, it would probably jump into somebody else, leaving a poor innocent person in jail for something they didn't do," Ember added.

"Right. Not good." DeeDee nibbled on a long clawlike nail. "Did you guys see anyone in that alley?"

Issy exchanged glances with her cousins. They shook their heads. "Nope. We weren't in there for a terribly long time, though. Why?"

"Ursula said Violet—that's the victim's name—must have been killed right before she was discovered. That corroborates the cook's testimony that Violet went out for a smoke and when she still wasn't back ten minutes later, the cook went to check on her slacking off and found the body. Must have stumbled on it right after it happened."

"Wow, then we must have just missed the killer," Ember said. "Oh. Wait, are you saying Owen suspects us?"

DeeDee smirked. "Nah. Not yet. You have no motive. Right?"

"Of course not. We didn't even know her."

"I didn't think so. Don't worry. Owen isn't as incompetent as you might think. In fact, he's actually pretty good. He's not some bumbling sheriff that is going to arrest the first person he thinks of without cause."

"That's good and bad," Raine said. "Good we won't be arrested, but bad that he might figure out who really killed Violet and arrest them, not knowing a demon was behind it."

"Yeah, hopefully you can make sure that doesn't happen, DeeDee." Issy gave her a pleading look.

"I'll try my best, but certain things are out of my control, and besides, I *do* have other things going on in my life besides trying to cover up the paranormal happenings in the town." DeeDee sniffed.

Ember's left brow quirked. "I have to say, you've been looking mighty fine lately, Miss DeeDee. Is there a special guy in your life you're getting all gussied up for?"

The wolf shifter's expression fell from a smile to a frown. "I wish things were that pleasant. Unfortunately, my father made a new alliance with another pack over in Vermont. To sweeten the pot, he made me part of the deal. My fun single days are almost over."

"What?" Gray made a face. "That's not right. Arranged marriages are outdated."

"For you witches, maybe. For werewolves, not so much. Our pack alphas have the power to do pretty much whatever they please, especially when it comes to members of their own family." DeeDee stared out over the lake for a moment before looking at Issy. "You're lucky, though. You get a second chance."

"What?" Issy's breath hitched. "Why?"

"You haven't heard?" DeeDee smiled. "That sexy hunk Dex Nolan is moving to Silver Hollow. Just rented himself a house and everything."

"Moving? Here?" Issy's words squeaked out of her constricted throat. Bella yipped sleepily and licked her chin. Sure, Raine had mentioned the possibility of the FBPI moving in an agent to keep an eye on the paranormal populace, but she'd never thought...

Hands shaking, Issy set Bella on the ground then wiped her damp palms on the legs of her jean shorts. As far as she knew, Dex had left Silver Hollow after the Drummond case fully convinced there was no paranormal activity in town. She thought she caught a subtle telepathic vibe from the dog. One of approval. Approval for what? Maybe for wanting to run as far from Dex Nolan as she could.

Ember reached over and patted Issy's hand, her smile wide. "We all saw the way you two looked at each other."

"Yeah, cuz." Raine waggled her brows. "Wouldn't hurt to persuade the guy over to our side either."

"Stop, okay?" Issy scoffed. "I'm not getting involved with an FBPI agent."

Gray set his empty plate aside then turned to DeeDee once more. "I'm really worried about Owen getting all gung-ho on this case. If this is a true instance of demon possession, then whoever killed that dishwasher can't be held responsible, because the demon is the real killer. But Owen is going to be looking for someone to arrest. I don't see how we can get around that."

"We'll have to think of something." DeeDee stared into the fire. "There's another problem too."

"What's that?" Issy asked.

"We found something else on the victim that might be a direct link that could send this innocent possessed person to jail."

"What?" Raine asked.

"A charm."

"Like from a bracelet?" Ember frowned. "There are tons of those out there these days. Doesn't seem like that would give Owen much information."

"Normally, I'd agree," DeeDee said. "But this one's distinctive—gold and enamel with a center stone."

Issy bit her lip. "But tons of people use that alley every day. Anyone could've dropped it, if he found it on the ground. Or it could even have belonged to the victim. Maybe she lost it during the struggle. What makes you think it's from the killer?"

"Because the victim wasn't wearing a bracelet," DeeDee said. "And we didn't find the charm on the ground. In fact, it was Ursula who found it during the autopsy."

The woods around them grew silent. Cosmo danced wildly beside Gray, the kittens screeched loudly and jumped into Ember's lap, and Bella cowered between Issy's ankles.

Not good. Not good at all.

"Where did she find it?" Issy whispered.

"Inside the wound." DeeDee's voice took on an ominous tone. "The only way it could've gotten there was during the murder."

Chapter Six

An hour after DeeDee left, the Quinn cousins still sat in their same spots as the campfire slowly died and storm clouds hovered over the peaks of the distant White Mountains. A pall had fallen over the group after the deputy's revelations.

Raine finally pushed to her feet and hauled Mortimer's pot up into her arms. "I need to head home."

"Not so fast, missy." Brimstone trotted around the corner of the house with something dangling from his mouth. As he got closer, Issy saw it was a police evidence bag. He dropped it near Issy's feet then hopped up on her log and stretched out lazily. "Check that out."

"Um, that's official police business." Issy shook her head. "No way I'm getting my fingerprints on that bag."

Brimstone halted mid-lick of one paw and gave her the feline equivalent of a give-me-a-break look. "Seriously? After breaking and entering for the Louella Drummond crime, you

52

really expect me to believe you're scared to touch a little bag? Come on. I stole it from Owen's office especially for you."

Raine put Mortimer back down. His leaves quivered and then bent toward the bag just as Raine leaned over and squinted at it herself. "Looks like something shiny."

"And glittering," Ember added, her gaze narrowed. "I see definite glitter."

As if the familiars sensed something important was in the bag, Bella's ears perked up with interest, and the kittens opened their eyes and lengthened their legs in a full stretch that made the little pink pads on their toes separate.

"*Woof.*" Bella barked happily, looking up at Issy as if alerting her to the importance of the charm.

"Yes, I see it. Are you trying to tell me something?"

Bella spun in circles, her tail jerking back and forth. Issy smiled. "Well, maybe she is coming along further than I thought."

Endora and Bellatrix trotted over and sniffed the bag then looked up at Ember, who smiled proudly at them. "Ditto here."

"Easy for them. They didn't have to do the hard work of procuring it. But I suppose someone has to show them how it's done." Brimstone glared at the other familiars, but Issy thought she saw a fleeting look of approval in his eye before he turned to her. "Now it's up to you humans to figure out how to benefit from it."

Issy pinched the edge of the bag between her thumb and forefinger and held it closer to her face. "Obviously, this must be the charm that DeeDee said Ursula found in the victim's wound."

The charm was a beauty. Glittering gold in the shape of a crown with sky-blue enamel, marred by dark smudges—blood, she assumed. Near the center sat a cushion-shaped turquoise-blue jewel.

Issy held it out. "Anyone recognize the design? Maybe if we can figure out the maker, we can figure out who purchased it."

"Never seen one like that before," Raine said, shaking her head.

"Me neither," Ember added. "From out of town maybe?"

"Well, there's only one way to find out." Gray plucked the bag away from Issy and held it in front of Cosmo. "Fly into town and compare this to what's in the jewelry store windows. Good boy."

The cockatoo took off in a flap of white wings, and the cousins sat back down again.

"Finally someone who takes action." Brimstone picked the bag up. "Have you seen enough? I need to return it before Sheriff Know-Nothing figures out it's gone."

"Fine. Go," Ember said, and they all watched him trot off, his dark-gray fur disappearing into the darkness of the forest.

"How long will it take Cosmo?" Issy shoved around the red-orange coals of the fire with a stick. "I've got to be in my store early tomorrow."

"Not long." Gray stretched out his long legs and stared up into the starry sky, now dotted with clouds. Issy, Raine, and Ember did the same. When they were kids, they'd lain outside on many a night, staring at the stars while their parents pointed out the different constellations, and looking up at them always comforted Issy.

After about twenty minutes, Gray said, "Do you guys ever think about settling down? Maybe starting a family?"

The three female Quinns exchanged a look.

"Why? Are you?" Issy smiled.

He opened his mouth, telltale splotches of red dotting his high cheekbones, and started to speak, but a loud screech stopped him. Cosmo swooped down onto Gray's shoulder, let out a triumphant squawk, then nuzzled Gray's ear.

"Okay. My beautiful boy here says the charm came from a new store on the south side of town called Charmed. Seems they specialize in these things."

"South side, huh?" Raine crossed her arms. "Puts an end to our investigation."

"No kidding." Ember scowled. "Wouldn't set foot over there if someone paid me."

"C'mon, guys." Issy sighed. Sure, the Quinns had had a long-standing feud with the coven who lived in that area of Silver Hollow. And yes, maybe the two sides didn't get along at all. But sometimes there were more important things than old disagreements. "I think a dead body outranks some silly feud, don't you?"

"What about all those dirty tricks they pulled on us when we were in school, huh?" Raine asked. "I didn't appreciate having every cornfield outside of Silver Hollow sprouting with the words 'For a Good Time Call Raine Quinn.'"

"Yeah, and that time they slipped an attraction spell into my Home Ec chocolate project? I fought off unwanted suitors for weeks because of them," Ember growled.

"Fine. Okay. They have poor taste in jokes, I'll admit. But I've never heard of them doing anyone any real harm or of them practicing dark magic. Besides, it sounds like if we want to find out who this demon has possessed and save an innocent person's life, then we have to go." Issy stood and placed her hands on her hips. "Now, who's paying a visit to Charmed with me tomorrow?"

Chapter Seven

It turned out, only Gray was able to take a break from clipping hair and go with Issy to Charmed the next day. Both Raine and Ember had called off, claiming they were far too busy to investigate again.

Issy had expected a bland little shop in some strip mall, but the store turned out to be a blissful stone cottage set in a mossy hillside covered with wildflowers. From the twittering birds, to the tinkling of a nearby brook, the whole scene seemed, well... textbook fairy-tale charming.

She pulled Brown Betty, her rusted-out pickup truck, to the curb and jammed the ancient transmission into park. Last night, she'd been pumped on adrenaline and raring to go. Today, though, sitting here on the wrong side of town, all she felt was hesitant. "Ready?"

"Sure," Gray said, glancing at her. "If you are."

"What if the owner recognizes us and kicks us out?"

"Look." He pointed out the windshield at the other cars lining the street. "Whoever's working in there isn't going to pull anything with so many witnesses around, especially if there are humans present. Everyone follows that rule. I think we'll be fine."

Exhaling loudly, Issy undid her seat belt. "Okay. If you say so."

"I do." Gray got out and met her on the sidewalk leading up to the store. Traffic into and out of the place seemed pretty steady. They made their way inside to the tinkling of bells above the door. The gentle scents of vanilla and lavender wafted through the air and helped ease Issy's nerves.

Maybe Gray was right. Maybe they had nothing to worry about, with all the tourists milling about the place, despite the nasty feud between their covens. A large orange tabby lazed atop one of the many glass display cases scattered around the shop. At the sight of Issy and Gray, however, the creature arched her back and hissed loudly.

And maybe Gray was wrong and they should get the heck out of there.

She took a step backward toward the exit just as the woman behind the register glanced up at them, her midnight-blue eyes widening. The name tag on her chest read Starla Knight, though Issy would've recognized one of the Knight Coven anywhere. And not just because of the telltale tingle she got in her gut whenever there was another paranormal in close proximity.

The blond woman's gaze darted around at the other customers nearby then returned to Gray and Issy. Her tone, though polite, held a definite edge of frost. "May I help you?"

Gray, for once, seemed speechless. He just blinked at the woman, unmoving.

Struggling to keep control of the tense situation, Issy took charge. After a deep breath for courage, she stepped up to the counter. "I'm sure you know who we are."

Starla eyed her warily. "I'd recognize a redheaded Quinn anywhere. What do you want?"

"I saw one of your charms recently," Issy said, ignoring Starla's defensive posture and instead perusing the collection in the glass case nearest her. "All of your designs are very unique."

"Yes." Starla said, looking from Issy to Gray then back again. "They bring good luck as well. But that still doesn't explain why you two are here. There's a perfectly good jewelry shop on the north side of Silver Hollow with comparable charms for sale."

"Not quite comparable." Issy tapped her index finger on the glass display case, which held charms almost identical to the one in the police evidence envelope. "These are different from anything I've ever seen. Very high quality and beautiful."

"Yes. Beautiful," Gray echoed.

Both Starla and Issy shot him a glance. What was wrong with him?

"Thank you." Starla's tone was appreciative but guarded. Issy thought she saw a little bit of the frost in the woman's demeanor melt, but it was probably just her imagination.

"Can I see them?" Issy asked.

Starla slid the door in the back open and pulled the tray out, setting it on the glass top. Issy leaned over. Yep. Same enamel, same stones. Different design but definitely the same charm that was found in the victim.

"Not afraid I'll put a hex on them?" Starla said, eyebrow raised.

"Oh." Heat prickled Issy's cheeks. Once, when they'd been ten, Starla had offered Issy a cupcake on the playground, and she'd thrown it away, at the encouragement of her cousins, telling Starla her family had probably cursed it. Those days seemed so long ago now and silly in retrospect. "I'm sure your items are fine."

"Hmm." Starla watched her for several moments before sighing. "If you'd like, I can put one on a bracelet for you so you can see how it looks on your wrist."

Starla gave Issy a tentative smile, and for a moment, Issy thought perhaps the Knights weren't so bad anymore. Perhaps someday she and Starla could even be friends. Then the childhood taunts, the evil tricks they'd played on Issy and her cousins reared their ugly heads, and Issy shoved the thought aside.

Her and Starla Knight friends? Maybe when toads tap-danced.

Issy tucked a long curl of her strawberry-blond hair behind her ear and bent over the display. "No, thanks. They're really beautiful, though. You must sell a lot of these, huh?"

"I do all right." Starla crossed her arms and surveyed the other customers. "Are you just looking, or are you actually going to buy something?"

Glancing up at Starla's sharp tone, Issy couldn't help wondering if perhaps Starla was the one possessed by the demon. After all, her moods seemed be swinging wildly from unaccountably nice to nearly hostile. According to the research she'd done last night, strange emotions and outbursts were also hallmarks of a possession, and those clever demons were known for letting their host "take control" when it was advantageous. She caught Starla's gaze once more and looked deep into her dark-blue eyes but didn't spot that dark, soulless demon victims usually displayed.

"That was some storm yesterday, huh?" Issy asked, thinking maybe she could trick Starla with a lie. Demon possessions were also known to cause memory loss in their human hosts.

"What storm?" Starla scowled. "Listen, I'm super busy and really don't have time to play games. If you want to see something, great. Otherwise, I've got other customers to serve."

Darn.

Issy was ninety-nine percent sure the charm found in the wound had come from this shop, but how many people had bought these charms?

"I'm looking for something completely unique for my aunt. She can be very particular. Doesn't want to end up with the same jewelry as her old cronies. Are there a lot of charms like these around? Maybe if I could be assured that one of her friends didn't have the same charm..."

Starla looked like she was getting suspicious. She snatched the tray away and put it back inside the case. "These aren't one of a kind. One-of-a-kind charms like this would cost thousands of dollars. My clientele doesn't have that kind of money, and I have no intention of telling you who purchased charms from me, so if you want something completely original, I suggest you try Schuller Jewelers down the street."

Sighing, Issy straightened. She'd figured Starla wouldn't be eager to just blurt out her customer list, but she'd had to give it a try. "Okay, maybe I'll try there."

"Whatever." Starla gave her a dismissive wave then glanced over at Gray once more before walking away to help a nearby human couple.

"C'mon," Issy said, grabbing her cousin's arm on the way out the door. He'd been uncustomarily quite the entire time, as though he'd been in some kind of trance, and moving his big body now was akin to hauling concrete. Finally, when he crossed the threshold of Charmed, Gray appeared to snap out of his stupor.

He shook his head then squinted into the afternoon sunshine. "We done already?"

"Yes." Issy continued on down the sidewalk toward her pickup then tripped over a crack in the pavement, nearly face-planting on the ground. Mumbling under her breath, she straightened and glanced through the front windows of Charmed. Starla Knight stood watching them through the front window, her lips quivering as if she was stifling a smile.

Heat prickled up Issy's cheeks as she continued on around the old truck.

Raine had been right.

Those south-side Knights weren't happy unless they were pranking somebody.

She climbed behind the wheel of Brown Betty then slammed the door behind her. "We've been here for twenty-five minutes."

"Seriously?" Gray shook his head and frowned, getting into the passenger side of the truck. "I swear we just walked in that place."

She glanced sideways at him. Gray had a sort of dazed look on his face, as though maybe Starla had hexed him or something. Or maybe, like most men, he just got all flustered in a store full of jewelry.

"Yeah, you seemed a bit... *preoccupied*." She buckled her seat belt and waited for Gray to do the same then started the engine and signaled before pulling out into traffic. "Anything you want to share?"

"No. Why?"

"Oh, nothing. You just seem kind of odd. Like maybe you were bewitched. Or maybe your interest in Starla Knight has changed since we were kids and she almost turned you into a toad."

Gray's nose scrunched, and he stared out the window beside him, scrubbing a hand through his hair. "My only interest in Starla Knight is to find that stupid charm, okay?"

"Well, for your sake, I hope that's true." Issy didn't miss the way her cousin kept looking back at the shop. Maybe Starla had zapped him with an over-hexed spell. "For all we know, Starla could be the demon."

"Starla's no demon. And even if she was, what would we do, huh?" Gray glanced at Issy again, his expression annoyed. "Remember, it's not the host's fault if they get possessed. Whoever killed that dishwasher is still innocent. The demon's the one to blame."

"Right." Issy made a left turn and headed toward the north side of Silver Hollow once more. "I just wish we'd found out something more, something that would put us closer to figuring out who the killer is."

"Did you get Starla's customer list?"

"No." Issy parallel parked along the crowded street near the town green about two blocks from Enchanted Pets. "Weren't you listening in there? I couldn't just come out and ask her, so I tried to weasel my way around it. There's no way she's going to tell us who bought those charms."

Gray unbuckled his seat belt then shifted to face Issy. "Well, she might not share it with us Quinns, but she'll have to share it with the police when they question her about that charm. Which means—"

"Owen."

"Yep." Gray winked. "Once our good sheriff figures out where that charm came from and requests the shop's list of buyers, he'll know who the killer is and try to prosecute them."

Issy slumped back in her seat. "But that person's innocent. Which means we'll have to come up with some way to throw him off track. Blame the killing on someone he'll never catch."

"Unfortunately, I need to get back to the salon," Gray said, getting out of the truck then leaning back inside his open window, his beefy forearms resting on the frame of the truck. "I say right now our best plan of attack is to figure out who bought the charm and banish the demon before it kills again. We'll have to worry about Owen later on." He looked at his watch. "Sorry. I need to go. I've got a perm coming in at two fifteen."

Issy waved as he darted away, then locked up Brown Betty before heading back toward her pet store. Gray made it all sound so simple—find the buyer, destroy the demon. Her instincts, though, told her it would be much harder than any one of them suspected.

Chapter Eight

Issy had just reached the corner and was ready to cross the street to Enchanted Pets when she nearly collided with a man carrying a full bag of groceries. Apparently, Gray wasn't the only one preoccupied.

"Oh dear. I'm so sorry," she said, holding her hand over her eyes to block out the sun, realizing too late it was Luigi Romano. Issy forced a smile. "Hello, Luigi."

"Hello." He peeked at her around his bag, his tone formal.

From the top of the sack, she spied large ripe tomatoes, a stick of pepperoni, and several green peppers. Hoping to distract him from asking any inconvenient questions, she asked, "Doing some cooking today?"

"I'm preparing a new pizza recipe this afternoon. Karen over at The Main Squeeze is giving me access to her big wood-burning oven. She said I can use her juice customers as a test audience for my slices."

"Hmm." She and Karen Dixon had their own past after what happened to Louella Drummond, but the last thing Issy wanted to do at that moment was remind Luigi of that. Besides, he and Karen were pretty close. In fact, according to local rumors, it had been Luigi who'd convinced the committee to let the local witch outcast set up her juice bar in the first place. Besides, Karen had turned out to be okay in the end. Heck, they'd practically even become friends.

"That's nice." Issy nodded then stepped around him, hoping to make a quick escape to her store. "Well, have a great rest of your day."

"Wait!" Luigi hurried along beside her, the sides of the long black coat he always wore flapping out in front of him. "I heard about that dishwasher killing, and I suspect it was done by a demon."

His words halted her in her tracks. She knew it had been too much to hope that he'd bought their story about the sulphur smell being from Becky. Now he suspected a demon was out, and he was sure to have Issy, Gray, and Enid as his top suspects.

Issy feigned innocence. "What makes you say that?"

"All of those power outages, to start with." He towered above her, casting a large shadow over the area where she stood. She shivered despite the late-summer warmth. "Then there was the smell of sulphur when I found you and Gray with Enid Pettywood, acting suspicious yesterday."

"Yeah, we thought that might be a demon but couldn't figure out how it got here. I guess summoning one is a big no-no with the committee, huh?"

Luigi made a face. "Yeah. The committee. They take a dim view of conjuring up demons."

"So you'd be wanting to find that person and report them, right? I mean, that is why you're here—to prosecute those doing illegal magic."

"What? Oh yeah. Prosecute. That's right. I guess a dedicated, proficient wizard would do that. Might up my standing with the committee."

Issy's eyes narrowed. The way he said that seemed to imply that his wizarding skills weren't up to par. She'd been under the impression that he was one of their best wizards, sent here to keep law and order because of that whole Vonner incident. As if one dark witch in town meant they were all bad. "Raise your standing? What do you mean?"

Luigi adjusted the grocery bag on his hip and scowled at her. "Nothing. I mean, it's not like I had a falling out with them or anything. You know, not everyone can cast top-notch spells or master enchantments of the elements, and not everyone wants to go around handing down dire sentences and prosecuting others. Sure, I know order must be kept and all, but some of us have other goals in life." He glanced into the grocery bag. "Besides, the committee doesn't want to be bothered with small stuff. They have bigger happenings on their minds."

"They do?" Maybe there was more to Luigi's presence in Silver Hollow than Issy and her cousins had thought.

"Sort of. Well, anyway. Enough said. Don't go thinking that just because I'm not focusing my full attention on finding whoever summoned it that you can hide the fact that there's a demon around, and don't go thinking I won't have to make sure the appropriate punishment gets handed down if things start to fall apart."

Pulse thudding loudly in her ears, Issy swallowed hard.

Luigi narrowed his gaze. "Okay there, Isolde?"

He was the only person who called her by her full name, and it always set her teeth on edge.

She took a calming breath and smoothed her hands down the front of her jean shorts. "Yes. Fine, thanks."

Then a large black 1970s-style sedan drove down the road, and what little decorum Issy had managed to muster evaporated. She'd never expected to see that car again, let alone its driver. Time seemed to slow as she squinted inside to see Dex Nolan behind the wheel.

Darn it all.

"Um, it was nice talking with you again, Luigi, but I've got to get back to my store." She rushed off without waiting for his reply, her only goal getting the heck out of sight before Dex spotted her and decided to stop for a chat.

After rushing back inside Enchanted Pets and sending her assistant home for the rest of the day, Issy played with Bella then tried working on her store tagline again. Working with words always relaxed her, and she needed all the Zen she could get at that moment.

"*Yip!*" Bella pawed at her leg. The little dog seemed excited, as though she wanted to tell her something.

"What is it? You can send thoughts to me. Go ahead." Issy screwed her eyes shut, ready to receive the telepathic transmission from her dog.

Inside her chest, a warm, fuzzy feeling started to emerge. Hope. Love. Tall. Wait, Tall? Was Bella trying to tell her that Luigi was coming?

The bells above the front door jangled, and she jerked her head in that direction, the warm, trance-like feeling of the bond between her and Bella broken.

"Yip!"

Dex Nolan was standing inside the entrance, scanning her shop. Her heart tumbled to her toes. Most of the time, she was able to rationalize away her previous reactions to the guy. After all, no one could be as gorgeous as she'd remembered him being, right?

But now, with him back in town, back in her shop, there was no denying it.

Dex Nolan was every inch as handsome as she'd remembered.

Every inch as dangerous to her heart too.

Bella must have had similar thoughts about him, but without all the reservations, because she bounded over and practically kissed his gray running shoes.

"Issy. Great to see you again." He bent down and rubbed Bella's stomach while the dog shamelessly wriggled on her back. "And you too, Bella."

"Hi," Issy said. At least he'd remembered the dog's name. That was a point in his favor.

He sauntered over, all lean muscled lines and sexy grin, and Issy steeled herself against his charms. He was the enemy. He worked for the FBPI. He'd been sent to spy on her and the other paranormals in Silver Hollow. Getting involved with him would be a huge mistake. The sooner she remembered that, the better.

Now, if someone would tell that to her rioting hormones, she'd be all set.

"Hi, Dex." She tucked her strawberry-blond curls behind her ear and gave him a small smile. "What brings you back to Silver Hollow?"

"Well," he said, leaning against her counter and looking entirely too masculine and sexy. "Not sure if you've heard, but I'm now a resident of your fair town."

Oh yeah. I've heard.

"How nice for you," she said instead. "Silver Hollow's a great place to make a home."

"Yeah, I really like it so far. My house feels a bit empty, though." He glanced at her, his gaze flicking to her lips before returning to her eyes. And darn if her mouth didn't still tingle from his not-that-long-ago kiss. Not good. Not good at all.

Thankfully, he turned away to face her shop again before she did something ridiculous, like leap over the counter and smooch him silly.

"I remembered your store and decided to come in and get myself a pet," he said.

"Great." Her tone said the exact opposite. Not that Dex wouldn't make an excellent pet parent, but his adopting a buddy from her store meant she'd probably be seeing a lot more of him. "Take a look around, and let me know when you find someone you like."

"Sure." He wandered down a few aisles, stopping to coo at a few occupants here and there, then lingered before the large vivarium to Issy's left. "What about this guy? He seems friendly."

Sure enough, Gordon, the bearded dragon, stood and waved to Dex from his perch. Flustered, Issy stumbled over her words. "Oh, well, he's kind of a special order."

"Too bad." Dex leaned closer and waved back. "He seems to really like me."

Darn it all if it wasn't true too. She'd expected Gordon to bond with one of the town's paranormals, not with an FBPI agent. Still, if the way the tiny dragon was waving and puffing out his beard was any indication, he wanted to go with Dex.

She wasn't ready to give up Gordon without a fight, though. She felt he was meant for a powerful witch, and what if she gave him to Dex and then that powerful witch showed up? Best to try to persuade Dex to take another animal. She did her best to steer him toward some of her less-exotic offerings near the back of the store. "What made you decide to move to Silver Hollow?"

"Eh, you know." He shrugged and followed her down the narrow aisle toward the cages at the back of the store. "Not much family left where I was back in Ohio, and the bureau really needed people in this area. I'd been here on the Drummond case and liked the town, so I figured why not?"

"Where are you staying?" She showed him several salamanders and toads and even a gecko, but it seemed Dex had his heart set on Gordon.

"Renting a bungalow over on the north end of town," he said then headed back to the vivarium. "Nope. I want him."

Resigned, Issy returned to the counter. "Okay."

She rang him up—he bought not only Gordon, but also the vivarium and enough food and toys to last a year, plus a spiffy blue leash to walk him. As much as she hated to admit it, Issy was impressed. He seemed genuinely concerned about taking the best care of his new pet, which was always a good sign. Maybe Gordon had chosen his best owner after all.

With a final wave, Dex headed for the exit with his arms laden with the glass tank, Gordon, and all of his supplies.

"Sure you don't need help?" she called.

"Nope." He gave her a grin and wink over the top of Gordon's vivarium. "I got it."

Gordon gave Issy a final wave, and the two guys disappeared down the sidewalk outside.

She stared after them, shaking her head. Dex was right. He most certainly did have "it."

No matter how Issy might wish otherwise.

Chapter Nine

Dex walked the short distance to his car and loaded the supplies in the trunk then placed Gordon carefully on the passenger seat, taking special precautions to buckle his enclosure in to prevent him from sliding off the seat.

As he climbed behind the wheel and slid on his sunglasses, he couldn't help remembering how great Issy had looked. He started the engine then signaled and pulled out into the late-afternoon traffic. His memories were of her being pretty and sort of fairylike, for lack of a better term, with her bouncy light-red curls and sparkling sea-green eyes. Those remembrances didn't do her justice, however.

Not to mention the fact that seeing her in person again made him feel all giddy inside. And for a guy like him, who always kept all his angles covered, it was more than a little unsettling.

Truth was, he wasn't entirely sure *why* he'd decided to move to Silver Hollow. He flicked on his signal again then made a right toward the northeastern part of town. Oh, he'd been truthful about not having much family left and nothing to really keep him in the Buckeye State. But the honest answer was, he could've lived anywhere. The FBPI had branches all over the country.

Honestly, he'd not been able to stop thinking about that kiss between him and Issy that day in the forest behind Louella Drummond's place. And when the bureau had posted a job for an agent to live full-time in Silver Hollow, well, he'd figured it might as well be him.

His old partner, Stan, of course, had thought differently.

Ugh. The thought of Stan setting foot again anywhere around here made him ill.

Stan would've tried to bring all these nice folks into Area 59, claiming they were paranormals or some such nonsense. Dex chuckled and made another turn, left this time. There wasn't any such thing as a paranormal anything. And, yeah, that fact might make his job cushy and redundant and just a tad boring, but hey... someone had to do it, right?

Besides, paranormal-craziness aside, he loved sinking his teeth into a good murder case. And this town in particular seemed prone to those. Take this new dishwasher killing, for instance. Whoever had done the deed had tried to throw law enforcement off their scent by leaving behind that weird little voodoo doll, but Dex refused to be deterred. The thought of tracking down the person responsible for the homicide had his blood zinging with adrenaline and excitement.

He needed to be quick about it, though, if he wanted to prevent anyone else from getting hurt on his watch. Familiar trepidation washed over him like sludge. He'd waited too long all those years ago with that kid, the one who'd been kidnapped. If only he'd worked harder, faster, better, maybe he could've stopped what happened.

Dex shook off his anxiety and glanced over at Gordon. The lizard had his paw on the glass now, as if raising it in solidarity to Dex's cause. Dex smiled and fist-bumped his new pet.

This time he wouldn't fail, because he couldn't fail.

Not again. Never again.

And really, in the end, that was also why he was here, and why he'd taken the job with the FBPI to begin with. To prove he could protect those entrusted to him, whether they called themselves paranormals or not. Except somehow Dex got the feeling that instead of protecting them from bad guys, he might end up protecting them from his own people.

As if on cue, his phone blared, and he looked to see that it was Stan. He pressed the hands-free button on the new gizmo he'd installed on the dash.

"Nolan. That you?" Stan's abrasive voice filled the car.

"Yes, Stan. You called my phone, so it's me."

"Right. I just wanted to check in. I've heard some rumblings about paranormal activity in Silver Hollow."

Dex glanced down at Gordon, who was puffing out his beard. "Really?"

"That's the buzz on the network of underground informants. Have you noticed anything going on out there?"

"Well, there was a murder. A dishwasher behind a restaurant."

"That's what I heard. The dishwasher dumpster murder." Dex could hear the excitement in Stan's voice. "It always starts with a murder. And murder is great because that gives us an excuse to detain suspects and bring them in. I'll pack my bags and get out there right away."

Dex's chest tightened. "No. No. Hold on. I can handle it for now. It could be a false alarm.

You know how the underground can be unreliable." The last thing Dex wanted was Stan out here, breathing down his neck. The guy was annoying. And creepy. "Besides, I heard you were on the Cincinnati Stabber case, and your skills are vital for that. I don't think anyone else can do that job as good as you, right?"

"Well... I don't know if I'd say that." Stan's voice was filled with pride, and Dex could picture him with his chest puffed out, his head inflating with a large dose of ego. "But if you think you'll be okay out there..."

"I'll be okay for now. I might need your help later on, though, so be prepared." Dex's lips curled into a smile. Stan was so easy to figure out.

"Well, if you're sure. But word is that pet store owner that we suspected last time might be in the middle of things. That Quinn girl."

"You don't say."

"If I were you, I'd keep her under close surveillance."

"Close surveillance. No problem."

"Okay, then, I'll send the appropriate message to the sheriff out there so that you can get official clearance for the case."

"Perfect." This call was working out better than he'd hoped when he'd first seen Stan's name. Dex couldn't wait to dig into the murder officially.

"Ten-four. And Dex..."

"Yeah."

"Try not to get distracted by that hot deputy, Clawson. She's a real tiger but totally out of your league."

Dex hung up. Stan had the hots for Clawson? Dex barely remembered what the deputy looked like. But with Issy around, any other girl was sure to be forgettable.

He made a right into his residential neighborhood, and several people waved to him as they walked their dogs or pushed their babies in strollers. Dex took a deep breath and exhaled slowly, releasing some of his inner tension. His assignment here was to pretend he worked for the regular FBI. Insinuate into cases when it was warranted while all the time blending in, getting to know the townsfolk. Once they let him into their circles, then he had a duty to report back on any paranormal activity.

The idea of "reporting in" on his neighbors didn't sit well with Dex, and normally he would never accept any such job. But, in this case, it was all good. There would be nothing to report since he doubted his neighbors had these mystical paranormal abilities that Dex was pretty sure didn't even exist. No harm, no foul.

Two blocks later, he pulled into the driveway of his white bungalow with the dark-green shutters. He hadn't had time to properly unpack his stuff yet, so the place was still littered with boxes everywhere. At least he had his bed set up and a couple of folding chairs, a coffee pot that worked, and cable TV. Hey, a man had to have his priorities.

Dex unloaded the supplies from the trunk then came around to get Gordon unbuckled and carry his vivarium inside. Funny, but the minute he brought his new bearded dragon companion inside, the place felt more like home. After getting the vivarium situated on the kitchen counter, he promptly filled Gordon's food and water bowls.

Pet settled, Dex leaned on the counter and watched the little guy eat, a tug of affection pulling at his heart. Hard to believe after such a short time, but he felt oddly connected to this town and these people, to the point of being oddly protective of them. Seeing Issy again was just a bonus. Now that he had a pet, he'd have an excuse to see her more often too. And even better, the FBI wanted him to keep an eye on her, so he'd just be doing his job.

Win-win all around.
Especially if it led to another fiery kiss.

Chapter Ten

Issy was just getting back into the groove of writing her slogan after Dex left when the bells above the door rang again.

"Was that Dex Nolan I saw leaving?" Ember raced into the store with her basket over her arm, Endora's and Bellatrix's eager faces peering out at Issy over the rim. "If so, you need to spill the beans."

Patiently, Issy set her supplies aside again and smiled. "Yes, it was Dex. No, nothing happened. Well, except he bought a pet. Gordon, my bearded dragon."

"Huh." Ember took the kittens out and put them on the floor to play with Bella, who yipped excitedly around her feet. "Interesting."

"There's nothing interesting about it. The guy's probably lonely, living in a house all by himself."

"Right." Raine came through the front door to join them. "We all live by ourselves, but you don't see us moving halfway across the country to live near someone we kissed once in the woods."

"It was one kiss, and it was no big deal, okay?" She never should've told her cousins about that stupid interlude with Dex. "Forget about it."

"We will when you do, cuz." Raine leaned over the counter with a grin. "Where's he living?"

"He said he's renting a bungalow on the north side of town."

"Huh." Ember exchanged a mischievous look with Raine then pulled a box of chocolates from her basket. Ember's shop, Divine Cravings, lived up to its name, touting the best candies and chocolates in the area. Not to mention that she dropped a secret enchantment into the recipe every once in a while. "Maybe we should make a Welcome Wagon house call."

Issy eyed the box suspiciously. "Or not."

It had only been a few weeks since the Drummond case, and her cousins had hinted at setting her up with Dex, and she wouldn't put it past them now to slip her and Dex some sort of love potion amidst a few milk-chocolate-covered caramels to help things along. Never mind that it was against their credo—they'd justify it somehow by saying they knew she really wanted it.

Issy knew her cousins only wanted the best for her. She was mad at herself for being so transparent that they'd noticed there was an attraction in the first place. And when she'd told them about the kiss, she'd thought Dex was gone for good. She had to admit, her heart had beaten a little faster when she'd found out he'd moved here, but she couldn't pursue it. She'd seen human-witch relationships fall apart before, and with Dex being part of the FBPI, there was no way things would work out. And she didn't want to start something with him that she knew would end in heartache. It wouldn't be wise.

"I'm insulted." Ember gave Issy a hurt look. "I would never bespell an unsuspecting person, let alone one of my own family. That's bad luck. Besides, it's not necessary anyway."

"Really?" Issy stepped back and crossed her arms, feeling unaccountably vulnerable. "And why's that?"

"C'mon, cuz." Raine scoffed. "It's obvious from the way you and Dex make googly eyes at each other that there's a spark."

"There is no spark, okay?" She turned away from the counter to straighten the already perfect items on a nearby shelf. "And I do not make googly eyes at him."

"Sure you don't." Raine walked over to talk to a tank full of toads.

"What happened when you went to Charmed?" Ember asked, changing the subject.

"Starla's the same as we remembered. A Knight prankster through and through. She tripped me on my way back out to my truck then laughed." Issy finished fussing with her merchandise before facing Ember once more. "Gray acted weird, though."

"Weird how?" Raine asked from across the room.

"It was like he was frozen in place or something right after we entered. He took one look at Starla and then... *boom*!" Issy shook her head. "If I didn't know better, I'd think he had a crush on her. Talk about googly eyes."

"Seriously?" Ember frowned. "I can't believe he'd fall for someone from the south side. You know we don't mix with Southies. Maybe she whammied him with a hex."

"Must have." Raine returned to the counter, her expression dark. "The Knight Coven's like our archenemy. Gray wouldn't even consider hooking up with one of them. That's a little too Romeo and Juliet."

"That's what I thought—probably another one of her pranks or something." Issy shrugged.

"I don't think Gray is interested in any kind of serious relationship anyway," Ember said.

"Oh, I wouldn't be too sure." Raine lifted the lid of a goldfish tank, pinched a large fish flake between her index finger and thumb, and held it over the water. An orange fantail she'd nicknamed Oscar raced to the top of the tank, puckered his fish lips, and took the food right out of her hand. "He's had a certain aura about him lately."

"I noticed that," Issy said. "He seems kind of lonely."

Ember's brows shot up. "Gray? No way. He's a ladies' man. Likes to play the field too much."

"Even guys like him need to settle down eventually," Issy said. "But not with one of the Knights."

"No, that would not do. Not at all." Ember pursed her lips, then her eyes lit up. "You know who I'd like to see him with? DeeDee."

"Yeah, they'd be perfect together. And I noticed them exchanging a few looks."

"After that full-moon ritual, they seem to have bonded somehow." Raine shut the lid on the goldfish tank and screwed the cap back onto the fish flakes. "I've heard that when a witch performs that ritual for someone, sometimes it enables you to see straight into each other's hearts. So maybe those looks are because DeeDee and Gray know a lot more about each other than we think they do. But I don't think there is anything romantic between them. I don't sense that kind of chemistry. It's more like they are old friends."

Ember's face fell. "Oh well. Anyway, we all heard her say that she's promised to someone else."

Raine made a face. "Blech. That would be the day I'd let someone promise me to some guy I didn't even know."

Ember shrugged. "It's their culture. Seems like she's resigned to it."

"Well, I hope he's at least hot looking." Raine sighed. "But we have more important things to deal with than Gray's and DeeDee's love lives. Did you find any of those charms at Charmed?"

"Yes. She has them there. Too bad, as Gray pointed out, we have no way of getting ahold of her customer list to find out who bought the particular charm in question."

"Hmm." Raine pulled out her phone and thumbed in a message. "Done."

"Done what?" Issy asked.

"Sent a message to DeeDee. Owen's bound to get that customer list at some point, and maybe she can let us know what's on it before Owen starts tracking people down." Raine slid the phone back into the front pocket of her overalls. "Was the shop busy?"

"It was pretty crowded. A lot of tourists shopping. Didn't see anyone buying those charms, though, so maybe that will help us. If they aren't very popular, there will be fewer people on the list. Maybe we can figure out who it is fast before the demon does something else. Speaking of which..." Issy turned to Raine. "Did you look through your class notes on demon possessions? Might help if we knew exactly what this thing was up to."

"Yes, I did, and I don't think you're going to like it."

"Why not?"

"Well, as we suspected, the demon is looking for a permanent human host. But in order for it to inhabit a human body forever, it needs to make certain concessions. Sacrifices, if you will. You can't just take a soul out of Hades and bring it up to earth without giving something in return."

"Sacrifices? That sounds so old-fashioned. What kind of sacrifices?"

Raine scrunched up her nose. "That's where my notes got a little messy. I wrote down something about how it had to trade three lives for its freedom. But you were right about it using the power of the full moon. In fact, it has a time limit—it has to deliver all the souls before the new moon, or it doesn't get to keep the body."

"So it has to kill three people." Issy's heart sank. "One down, two to go."

"And they have to have something in common. In the book, it said something about virgins. You know, virgin sacrifices."

"So the dishwasher was a virgin?"

"I'm not sure about that. I think the whole virgins thing goes back a few hundred years. Might be something different now." Raine smirked. "Otherwise, the demon might have a hard time finding two more virgins in this day and age." Then her face turned serious again. "Sorry, that wasn't funny. Anyway, the three dead just have to have some similarity."

"If we could figure out what that might be, maybe we could figure out who it intends to kill next and stop it before someone else dies," Ember suggested.

Raine nodded. "Right. So, dishwasher... umm, maybe it will go for a sous chef next."

Issy made a face. "Really? What, you think Lucifer is down there starting a restaurant?"

Raine shrugged. "It was just a suggestion."

Issy sighed. "This is worse than I thought. Now we know the demon is going to kill again and it needs two more people in four days. Since none of us knows the first victim, we don't have much of a chance of figuring out the common thread he might be after. That leaves one option. We need to find the demon or, more precisely, who the demon is inhabiting."

"So we're right back where we started. With no clues, unless DeeDee can come up with that list fast," Raine said.

"Not exactly. We know one thing. Whoever the demon has taken up residence in wore that charm. That's the kind of charm that people like to collect. You know, different ones that have meaning to them. Then they load them up on a bracelet piece by piece," Issy said. "So it's likely our demon is still wearing the bracelet but with just one less charm."

"You know what we could do." Ember scooped up Bellatrix and cuddled her under her chin, the activity causing Endora to immediately halt playing with the catnip mouse she'd torn from the display rack and scamper over to Ember's feet, seeking her own attention.

"What?" Issy and Raine asked in unison.

"We could conjure a finding spell and cast it on all the charms sold from that shop in this vicinity. That way, we can observe the wearers for any strange activity."

"I don't know." Issy gave her cousin a skeptical look. "I thought you said you didn't bewitch anyone without their knowledge."

"It's not bewitching, and those charms aren't people. It'll be a piece of cake." She opened the box of candy she'd brought and popped one of the caramels into her mouth. "Or chocolate."

"Cool." Raine took a piece of candy too. "What should Issy and I do?"

"Once the spell is cast, we'll just need to sit and wait for the charm's owner to pass by." Ember smiled. "Anyone know a good spot?"

"How about The Main Squeeze?" Issy said. "We can sit on the outdoor patio."

"Perfect." Ember gathered her kittens from the floor and patted Bella's head before heading for the front door again with Raine in tow. "See you guys later."

Chapter Eleven

The Main Squeeze was as busy as always when Issy arrived. Bella pranced along beside her, her new silver-and-rhinestone leash sparkling in the sun. They waited at the back of the short line to order, and Issy pulled her buzzing phone from her purse.

"Oh darn," she said to Bella, who looked up at her, panting, her little pink tongue sticking out. "Raine and Ember are both going to be late."

Bella yipped then stood on her back legs, begging to be picked up.

It was humid this afternoon. Issy gathered her little dog into her arms. She'd need to get a bottle of water for Bella as well as a juice for herself when they got to the counter.

"Welcome to The Main Squeeze. May I recommend our Pomegranate Pleasure today, Issy?"

Issy glanced up to find Karen Dixon, the juice bar's owner, watching her closely. They'd had a bit of a rocky patch over the whole Louella

Drummond thing, but both women had agreed to put that behind them and start fresh. Issy gave her a small smile. "Hi, Karen. Looks like business is good."

"Business is great, thanks." She tossed her long straight black hair over her shoulder. "So how about it? The Pomegranate Pleasure is today's special and guaranteed to spice up your love life."

With Dex hanging around Silver Hollow again, she didn't need any more trouble in the love-life department. "Actually, I think I'll try your Pineapple Express with Celery, please. Oh, and a water for Bella."

"Sure thing." Karen rang up her purchase then handed Issy her change. "Should be ready for you at the other end of the counter."

"Thanks." Issy grabbed her order then chose an umbrella-shaded table near the edge of the patio. Even without her cousins present, it would be best to cast Ember's spell now, before the after-work rush began. That way she could start watching for anyone wearing one of Charmed's bracelets.

She sat Bella down and poured water into the paper bowl Karen had provided, then leaned back in the chair and admired the little dog. She thought she felt a little flutter of appreciation and wondered if it was a telepathic thought from the pup. Good, she was coming along just fine.

Water. Good.

"Yes, it is good!" Issy said, and Bella fixed her luminescent brown eyes on her and thumped her tail happily as if she, too, recognized that they were making progress in the witch-familiar bonding process.

Tall. Dark. Handsome. Good.

Wait. What? Issy narrowed her eyes at the dog, who was still looking pleased with herself. Had she just communicated... No. Must have been Issy's imagination.

Remembering the task at hand, she pulled out her phone to scan the spell Ember had texted. Looked simple enough. Now all she had to do was cast it without drawing too much attention.

Bella turned back to lapping up her water, apparently done with telepathic communications for the moment. Issy closed her eyes and took a deep breath then clenched her fists—focusing on Ember's enchantment over and over in her mind, building the energy levels within her then...

"*Invenieto!*" She whispered the magic word and released her fists. Tiny iridescent sparks flew from her fingertips.

Nervous, Issy glanced around to make sure no one had witnessed her little magic show. Tourists milled about along with other paranormals, but none of them gave her a second look. A couple strode by eating matching ice cream cones, a tiny toddler between them.

All right, then. Good.

Issy settled back in her chair to charm-watch and spotted Enid Pettywood coming out of the hat store across the green, Becky trailing along on a leash beside her. Enid raised her hand and waved. Issy waved back then watched the two continue on down the street.

Bella finished her water then circled around three times before lying down on the ground near Issy's feet, only to jump up again and bark wildly as an orange-striped tabby slinked by. Brimstone followed close behind the strange feline, as if tailing it.

The cat stopped near Issy's table and looked behind to where Brimstone had been, just seconds before, but there was no sign of the large charcoal-colored familiar now. The cat looked up at Issy and held her gaze for a moment, its green eyes narrowed, then continued on down the block.

Something niggled at the back of Issy's memory. There was something familiar about that cat. But she was distracted when Brimstone emerged from a nearby doorway, as if he'd been hiding, and followed after the tabby. He winked at Issy as he passed her table.

That was odd.

Issy glanced to her left again and then realized why the orange tabby seemed familiar. It was the tabby she'd seen at Charmed, and her owner was not far behind.

Starla Knight's gaze darted around nervously, and her steps were uncertain as she hurried down the street across from the juice bar. A charm bracelet jangled on her wrist.

Starla raced forward, head down and expression grim—as though she couldn't wait to escape this side of town—and, once again, Issy couldn't help wondering if Starla was the one possessed by the demon. She was wearing a bracelet with charms, for sure, but were they the fancy enamel charms found on the murder victim, and was one of them missing?

There was only one way to find out, and now seemed as good a time as any to ask.

Except before Issy could get up, Gray ran out of Sheer Magic and headed straight for Starla. They stood about fifty feet from where Issy sat... and *newt shizzle*. It was too far for Issy to hear what they were saying. She contemplated a lip-enunciation spell, but they'd both know she'd bewitched them and would move out of range.

What in the world is going on with them?

"Hey, Gordon. Look who's here!"

Issy swiveled fast to see Dex smiling down at her, his new pet waving at Issy like always. She glanced back at her cousin and Starla before grinning up at Gordon and his owner. "Hi, guys. How are you today?"

"Great, thanks." Dex rambled on about getting settled in his house and making Gordon feel comfortable, but Issy was only paying half attention because Gray and Starla were still heavily into their conversation, and in the distance, Raine and Ember approached from across the green. So she nodded and made noncommittal noises while she tried to figure out what Gray was up to and hoped her cousins would not notice that Dex was standing at her table.

The next time she glanced at Dex, he was watching her expectantly, as though he needed an answer and... and... and...

Oh, darn.

If her cousins caught her and Dex talking, they'd question him endlessly, and Issy would never hear the end of it. So her first order of business was to get him out of here. Fast.

"What do you say?" he asked, his hazel eyes hopeful. Gordon waved to her again, and between the cute lizard and the gorgeous guy, Issy figured whatever he'd asked her couldn't be that bad, right?

So she nodded. "Sure. Okay."

"Fantastic!" Dex took a step back. "I'll call you later, then, to set up dinner. And maybe we can discuss whether I should take my main lizard man here in the shower with me and what treats are best to feed him too, eh?"

"What?" Issy frowned, looking from Dex to her cousins, who were now just across the street. Had she agreed to have dinner with him? Dinner with Dex, alone, hadn't been on her radar, but she needed to get rid of him. Now. "Sounds awesome."

"Cool!" Dex backed away from her, his hand raised in direct imitation of Gordon. "Talk to you later, then."

"Yep." Issy waved, exhaling as he finally left just as her cousins approached. Luckily, Raine and Ember were intercepted by Enid Pettywood mid-street, which gave Issy a moment to compose herself. What had she done? Dinner with Dex? She covered her face, and Bella licked her ankle in sympathy.

"What did Mr. Hottie want?" Ember asked as soon as they sat down.

"Got yourself a date, cuz?" Raine gave her a knowing smile as she took the place across from Issy.

Yes. "No." Issy took a sip of her surprisingly yummy juice drink. No wonder Karen's business was booming. "Dex wanted pet advice, that's all. Are Gray and Starla still behind me?"

Ember leaned to the side then shook her head. "Starla Knight? What would she be doing on this side of town?"

"No idea." Issy gulped down more of her juice. "She was headed toward me, then Gray came running out of Sheer Magic and stopped her. They stood back there for quite a while, talking. Then Dex came and—"

"And you got distracted," Raine finished for her. "Hormones. It's okay, cuz. We all have them."

"Speaking of hormones." Ember pointed toward Gray's hair salon. "Here he comes now."

Gray charged out of Sheer Magic once more, Brimstone at his heels, and headed for their table. He took a seat beside Issy, looking oddly frazzled for a guy who prided himself on his perfect appearance.

Issy leaned closer to him, suspicious. After what had happened to him in that charm store and now this, she was even more worried that Starla had hit him with some sort of damaging hex or charm. "What was up with you two back there, huh?"

"Nothing." Gray scowled down at his hands on the table. "She contacted me and said she wanted to meet. It was weird. I thought she might be up to something, but she said she heard about the murder and got the strongest urge to talk to *me* about it. Said she wanted to help and figured that's why we were in her store looking at the charms. Asked all kinds of questions about the charm and how it was connected to the murder."

"Right." Raine sat back, clearly skeptical. "Chances are good she has another agenda, and we shouldn't believe a word she says. She is a Knight, after all."

"Yeah, we can't trust her." Issy leaned forward and picked an orange hair off Gray's shirt then held it up to the light to inspect it.

Gray scowled at the hair. "That orange tabby we saw at the store was with her. Meowing and causing all kinds of bad vibes. That cat seems bossy."

"Sounds like someone else I know." Issy cast a pointed glance at Brimstone. "But I wouldn't put too much stock in anything Starla Knight said. She's probably trying to cast suspicion on someone else. I noticed that she was wearing a charm bracelet and has been acting out of character. Maybe it's her that is possessed."

Gray shook his head. "I don't think so. She seemed sincere. Said she knew we didn't always get along, but the Southies don't want a demon loose any more than we do, so she felt compelled to tell me who bought the charm."

Issy, Ember, and Raine exchanged a look. They were all thinking the same thing. Starla might have bewitched Gray in order to get him on her side.

"She told you who bought it?" Ember asked.

Gray's face turned grim. "Nikki Pettywood."

"Oh dear." Issy slumped back in her chair. "She was there that morning when Enid summoned the demon too. She headed for the pub right before Enid got stuck."

"Yeah," he said. "She seemed pretty tipsy already too, when I was cutting her hair. Alcohol makes people more susceptible to possession. Lower inhibitions and all."

"Especially when they are passed out drunk like Nikki was yesterday afternoon behind O'Hara's pub," Brimstone said.

The cousins turned to look at him.

"What? A cat has to carouse, and there's no better place than the alley beside O'Hara's, despite the greasy smell of french fries and the disgusting aroma of sage burgers or the stench of rotted lettuce." Brimstones whisker's twitched. "They need some new fish items on the menu, I tell you. Anyway, Nikki was dead to the world... no pun intended. Even loud police sirens couldn't wake her, and you know how demons love to inhabit people who are unconscious. Easy pickings."

"Still doesn't explain why Starla would want to help us," Ember said.

"If I had to guess"—Raine sat forward, scowling—"I'd say she's setting us up to owe her big time later. Those Knights never do anything without expecting something in return."

Issy rubbed her eyes. This day had somehow taken a downward spin. Her chest pinched at the thought of poor Enid all alone. What if her granddaughter went to prison for murder? "Well, even if that's the case, it does seem like there's a good chance that Nikki is hosting the demon."

"Maybe, but are we going to go by what Starla Knight tells us?" Raine asked.

Issy shrugged. "If we could find some way to get the demon out of Nikki that wouldn't harm an unpossessed person, maybe that would be worth a try."

"Right, hedge our bets," Raine said. "Get rid of the demon if she is possessed, and no harm if not. Worth a try."

"Yeah, but how do we get it *out* of her?" Gray asked.

"A potion," Ember said. "No self-respecting demon will drink one, but I can put it into a special batch of my chocolates. Maybe infuse some soft maple centers. Those are Nikki's favorite. She comes into Divine Cravings all the time to buy them."

"Okay." Issy picked up Bella, who was dancing around her ankles. "What supplies do you need to make it?"

"I've got everything I need except briarwort fern." Ember turned to Raine. "Do you have any in your greenhouse? It's pretty rare."

"Nope. I know where I can dig some up, though." Raine stood and adjusted the straps of her green overalls. "I'll go out into the woods right now."

"Awesome." Ember pushed to her feet as well, the twirly skirt of her frilly sundress swishing around her legs. "I'll go back to my shop and get the molds for the candies and the other ingredients ready."

"Great," Gray said. "I've got to get back to my shop. Tonight's my late night in the salon. When are we doing this?"

Issy took another sip of her juice. "Tomorrow. Two p.m. Enid told me once that Nikki always visits her every day at that time for afternoon tea. We can drop by and give her the chocolates without anyone thinking twice about it."

Chapter Twelve

The next day, Issy tended shop at Enchanted Pets while Hannah went to lunch. She fiddled with her outfit for the umpteenth time while attempting to work on her slogan. Hard to believe she'd spent way too much time this morning picking out this stupid skirt and top that itched and felt too tight in all the wrong places and...

Ugh. Just ugh.

If she was honest, her discomfort had nothing to do with her clothes and everything to do with the fact that she'd agreed to go on a date with Dex Nolan. The whole thing still seemed a bit unreal, especially since she hadn't even realized she'd agreed to it, what with being so preoccupied with Raine and Ember coming toward them.

She probably could have wriggled her way out of it, but he'd called her last night, and they'd ended up talking for over an hour—covering every subject from Gordon's care to music to movies—and she hadn't even realized the time.

Darn if he wasn't interesting and cute and everything she wanted in a guy. He'd even offered to take her to this new French bistro in the next town over, the one she'd been dying to try since it opened three months prior. How was a girl supposed to refuse an offer like that?

She hadn't, and that was the problem.

And not her only problem at the moment either. Not by a long shot.

Normally a solid sleeper, Issy had tossed and turned all night, unable to forget Dex's sunny smile or their previous kiss—*oh holy toads*—that kiss. Her lips still tingled every time she thought about it.

Issy sighed and covered her face with her hands.

Then there was also the upcoming meeting with Nikki and Enid as soon as Hannah returned. Dread settled heavily in her stomach like a bowling ball. What if they couldn't get Nikki to eat Ember's chocolates? What if the potion wasn't strong enough to drive out the demon? What if it wasn't even in Nikki? What if...

"Hey, cuz." Raine came through the door of Enchanted Pets. "Ready?"

"Not yet." Issy glanced at the clock. "It's only one thirty. I have to wait for Hannah to get back first. She should be here in about five minutes."

"Fine." Raine scratched her arm then winced. "I'm going to wait outside. I got a rash from picking the briarwort, and the sun helps. Plus, Ember gave me a couple of Benadryl to stop the itching."

"Okay."

Issy watched her cousin walk back out to her Jeep, parked near the curb, then climb inside. Raine had worn something other than her usual overalls today too—a pair of dark-blue jeans and a long-sleeved black top. The sleeves, Issy knew, were to cover the rash. They didn't call those ferns briarwort for nothing. They carried lethal-looking stickers that left their poor victims covered in awful welts.

She checked the clock again then squinted out the front windows into the early-afternoon sunlight, spotting her assistant crossing the street and heading for Enchanted Pets.

Perfect. Right on time.

At least one thing today seemed to be going properly.

Hannah came in, and Issy quickly gathered Bella and did a final check of her hair in the mirror before hurrying outside to join Raine and the newly arrived Ember in the Jeep. Bella seemed desperate to play with Ember's kittens, so Issy gave in and secured her in the backseat with the tiny cats instead of holding her on her lap as usual. "Where's Gray?"

"He's not coming," Raine said then yawned. "Said he's booked solid for the afternoon."

"You okay to drive?" Issy asked, concerned. Anytime she'd taken Benadryl in the past for allergies, it was like getting shot with a tranquilizer gun.

"Yeah, I'm fine." Raine signaled then pulled out into traffic. They all waved as they drove past Sheer Magic. "I'll be better, though, once these stupid hives go away."

"Well, if you need me to drive, just let me know," Ember said from the backseat. Her kittens peeked over the rim of the basket on the seat beside her.

It was a short drive to Enid's small cottage, and they made it there with ten minutes to spare. Raine parked under a large shady oak tree. Issy unbuckled her seat belt and glanced back at Ember. "You have the candy?"

"Right here. Maple creams for Nikki, and raspberry creams for Enid." Ember held up two gold-foil-covered boxes.

"And you're sure they won't hurt Nikki if she's not possessed?" Issy asked.

"Relatively sure. I mean, it won't cause any permanent harm, just minor side effects like upset stomach, flu-like symptoms. Nikki is young, so she can handle it. Enid is older and might have a more severe reaction, which is why I brought her the raspberry creams."

"And if Nikki is possessed, how will we know it worked?"

"There should be a sign. Some kind of electrical disturbance," Raine said. "At least that's what it said in my class notes."

"Okay, then." Issy studied her cousin. "Raine, are you sure you're okay?"

"Yes. I'm good." She stifled another yawn then got out and walked around to wait for them on the sidewalk while the ladies made sure their familiars were happy and content to remain in the open-air Jeep while they went inside. Issy didn't want to take the chance of Bella or the kittens being injured by the rogue demon harbored inside Enid's home, and neither did Ember.

Once they were sure Bella and the kittens couldn't get out but still had enough air from the open top, they both joined Raine.

Together, the three Quinn cousins walked up to the door and knocked.

Enid answered, her smile broad. "Oh, what a lovely surprise! Nikki, dear, come see who came to visit us today!"

Nikki peeked her head around the door, her gray, slightly bloodshot eyes widened. "Oh, hi."

"We hope it's okay to drop by unannounced, but we thought it would be nice to spend some time together," Issy said. "Right, Raine?"

"Yep." Raine agreed.

"And we brought treats!" Ember held up her boxes of goodies. "May we come in?"

"Of course! Please." Enid stepped aside and let them into her quaint little home. "Let's go into the kitchen. My granddaughter and I were about to have tea. Won't you ladies join us?"

"Sure." Issy watched Nikki carefully as they walked through the tidy living room bedecked with doilies and crochet and headed into the kitchen. For a woman possessed, Nikki Pettywood didn't show any of the outward signs. In fact, with her plain T-shirt, jean shorts, and flip-flops, she looked more like one of the town's many tourists than a dangerous paranormal. She wasn't wearing her charm bracelet today either —or any other jewelry, for that matter. Had Issy heard something about demons not liking the feel of precious-metal jewelry and stones on their skin? Then again, Enid didn't seem to be wearing any either, so maybe the Pettywood women just didn't like to get all jeweled out when they were just having their usual afternoon tea.

They all took a seat around Enid's dining table, and Ember set the chocolates in the center of the table. "I brought your favorite, Nikki. Maple cream centers." She slid one package toward Nikki then the other toward Enid. "And I brought you raspberry cream."

Both Nikki and Enid unwrapped the boxes. Enid plucked out a raspberry cream, popped it into her mouth, and made nummy noises.

Nikki shoved two maple creams into her mouth. The cousins all exchanged a look, and Issy slipped her hand into her purse and curled her fingers around the smooth obsidian talisman she always kept nearby for both comfort and protection. She wasn't exactly sure what kind of energy would be flying around when the demon left Nikki's body, and she wanted to be ready.

Nothing happened.

Nikki stuffed a third into her mouth then looked at the cousins, her cheeks full. She slid the box toward them and mumbled, "Would you like one?"

The three cousins shook their heads.

"I would. I like maple creams too." Enid reached across the table toward Nikki's box.

"I brought the raspberry creams for you." Ember's voice squeaked with anxiety as she pushed the raspberry cream box closer to Enid and pulled the maple creams farther away.

"Yes, but I like them both. Don't worry, I'll share the raspberries with Nikki." Enid grabbed the maple cream box again.

"You don't want one of those—" Issy tried to shove the box away.

Enid gave her a funny look and swatted her hand away. "Whyever not? They look just as delicious as the raspberry creams."

Before Issy could stop her, Enid plucked a candy out of the box and ate it.

Ember tensed beside Issy as they watched Enid chew.

They all stared as Enid ate another one. "Yes, these *are* tasty."

Before they could stop her, she'd gobbled down three more in short order.

Then, suddenly, Enid frowned and grabbed her middle. "Oh, I don't feel so good."

The lights around them flickered.

"Uh-oh..." Raine said.

"Oh, no worries." Enid looked up at the overhead light. "Just more of the crazy electrical disturbances we've been having around town. You know, someone really should talk to the electric company—"

Her words were cut short when the lights winked out. Enid's kitchen was at the back of the house, shaded by trees, and she had the kitchen curtains drawn tight on the door and window. She must have had room-darkening shades since it was downright murky in there without the lights even though it was mid-afternoon.

"Oh my!" Enid said from the shadows. "I feel a little…"

"Gram!" Nikki cried. "Are you okay?"

Nikki stood from her chair and lurched toward Enid, who was now slumped over, but Nikki must have tripped. She fell, and her chair clattered to the floor, and then…

Kaboom!

The table shook, then the lights came back on. Nikki jumped up from the floor. Enid sat upright, a slight frown on her face.

Apparently, the maple creams had had a delayed effect. But Issy felt a flurry of satisfaction—the electrical happenings had proved the demon had been in Nikki and now was vanquished. Her satisfaction was tempered with a tinge of disappointment. She had been hoping just a little that Starla was the one possessed. Oh well, as long as the demon was gone now. She just hoped that Enid hadn't been badly harmed in the process.

"*Belch!*" Enid's hand flew to her mouth. "Oh, excuse me. That wasn't ladylike at all."

Nikki righted her chair then turned concerned eyes on Enid. "Gram, are you all right?"

"Never better, dear." Enid stood then looked around her, as if seeing the place for the first time. "Excuse me, but I need to get to my bridge game."

"No, Gram." Nikki glanced at Issy, her voice fearful. "That's on Monday. Today's Thursday."

"Oh." Enid appeared confused. "I guess time has slipped by."

Issy contemplated Nikki. Her eyes were clear, and she appeared to be genuinely concerned about Edith. Issy doubted she'd be able to fake that level of concern if the demon were still in her. Thankfully, Enid seemed relatively unharmed other than the bout of indigestion. "Maybe we should leave. Sounds like your grandmother needs some rest."

"Yes." Ember pushed to her feet as well, inconspicuously grabbing the box of maple creams from the table before any more could be consumed. "I need to get back to my shop."

"Me too," Raine said.

"I'll show you out," Nikki said. "Gram, you stay here."

"Okay, dear," Enid resumed her seat and grabbed a raspberry cream from the box.

"Thanks for coming by." Nikki held the door for them while the three of them scooted out.

"You're welcome. Nice to see you," Issy waved and moved in between Nikki and Ember, who was trying to hide the box of chocolates.

Nikki closed the door, and they skedaddled to the Jeep, Raine lagging behind, still sluggish from the Benadryl.

"I'll drive." Ember held her hands out for the keys, and Raine gave them over willingly and hopped in back with Bella and the kittens.

"Thanks. I guess that medicine is affecting me worse than I thought." Raine pulled up her sleeves to show the weepy scratches. "Isn't working either. These are still itchy."

"Those briarwort scratches itch something terrible. I had them once when I was a kid," Issy said.

"I remember." Ember buckled her seat belt then waited while Issy did the same. "The Knights made fun of you too. Called you Itch-a-Long Cassidy."

"Yep." One more reason to dislike the Knights. No compassion whatsoever. They turned off Enid's tree-lined boulevard and headed toward downtown Silver Hollow. "Sorry the Benadryl isn't working, Raine. I think we had better luck with the potion in the candies working, though. That's what caused the power to go out, right?"

"I think so." Ember shrugged. "I'm no demon-exorcism expert or anything. I just mix the potions to the best of my abilities."

"I hope poor Enid will be okay too, after eating those chocolates," Issy said. "She seemed to have some indigestion and memory loss. What will you do with the rest of them?"

"I need to de-charm them. Then they'll be fine for anyone to eat. I think Enid will be okay, but maybe you should call and check on her tonight, to be sure."

"Oh, right." That would give her an excuse to cut her evening with Dex short too, which was good. Too much time in that man's presence might be detrimental to her willpower.

"I'll get with Gray later and see if he can help me keep an eye on Nikki. See if she goes anywhere or does anything suspicious."

Issy nodded. "Sounds like a plan. Good luck trying to get Gray out of his shop, though. He seems crazy busy these days."

"I know, right?" Ember pulled up outside Enchanted Pets and nodded at Raine, who was snoozing in the backseat, her head tilted back and mouth wide open. "I'll take Raine back to her house and get her into bed then call a cab to pick me up."

"Don't be silly." Issy unclipped Bella's leash from the seat belt harness then straightened with her tiny dog in her arms. "You head to the cabin, and I'll follow behind you in Brown Betty."

"You sure?"

"Absolutely." Issy smiled. "We Quinns have to stick together, right?"

Chapter Thirteen

Dex had seen his share of small-town police buildings, and the one in Silver Hollow actually wasn't too shabby despite the small size of the town. Sure, it wasn't abundant in space—none of them were—but it had a decent-sized lobby and a few cells. The evidence room could have used some work or maybe a lock on the door, but that wasn't Dex's problem. He supposed the lax attitude toward security worked here. After all, how many real crimes could this small town have?

Then again, there had been two murders just this summer.

One thing he wished—especially if there were going to be more murders here—was that they would enlarge the sheriff's office. It was tiny, and now—just as in the previous murder case—Dex found himself stuffed in there with three other people, raising the temperature to balmy and making the air thick.

Owen didn't have much furniture, just a plain metal desk with a 1950s green Pleather chair behind it and a hard plastic guest chair that no one, including Dex, wanted to sit in. Right now, Owen was standing behind the desk, and the medical examiner, Ursula Lavoie, stood across from it. DeeDee Clawson was leaning against one wall, and Dex leaned against the wall opposite her. Dex's official involvement in the case had been sanctioned by the FBI, and Owen had called the meeting to bring everyone up to date on the clues and ME findings.

Dex studied the others as Owen rattled off the specifics of the case and Ursula talked medical speak. The sheriff looked more as though he belonged on a surfboard, though Dex could see his face was set in grim determination. In the murder case earlier this summer, Dex hadn't been too sure about Sheriff Gleason, but now he realized that even though the guy wasn't super savvy about police work, he certainly had the desire. And he seemed like a fair man carefully considering all the clues and not wanting to jump to conclusions and throw the book at everyone, as Stan would have done. Now that Dex was thinking about it, he'd much rather work with Owen than Stan.

Dex had met Detective Clawson—DeeDee, as the locals called her—during that earlier case too. But now she looked different. He wasn't sure what it was—surer of herself and... well... more attractive. Maybe they'd gotten new deputy outfits or she'd had her hair cut. It didn't really matter. What did matter was that Dex liked her. He got the distinct impression she was "on his side," though he had no idea why. As far as he knew, there weren't any sides for anyone to be on.

The other woman was even stranger than Gleason and Clawson. She looked as though she spent a lot of time in the morgue. Her hair, a stark jet black, was pulled back tight in a bun at her neck. Her skin was as pale as ivory soap, and her eyes were as dark as her hair. But the kicker was her ruby-red lips—a splash of bright color in her otherwise pale demeanor. Dex supposed she was pretty but not in the same way that Issy was.

Thoughts of Issy made his chest constrict. He was looking forward to their date that night.

Date?

The word signified the beginning of a relationship. Dex didn't want to admit how much he hoped that was what it was. He didn't like the funny feeling of being out of control that surfaced when he was around her. Yet he couldn't stay away from her. And if there was a dangerous killer in town, he wanted to make sure Issy was in no danger. But that was only one of the reasons he was eager to help on the case. The other was that he wanted the chance to put his detective skills to use. Hanging around town and looking for nonexistent paranormals was pretty boring.

Stan had called him again the night before, wanting to know if he'd witnessed any paranormal activity. He'd been excited about the various power outages around town. Dex had been overcome with a strange feeling of protectiveness for the people of Silver Hollow and had told Stan the power outages had been traced to a faulty transformer. It was the first time he'd ever lied on the job, but he felt justified in it because Stan's witch hunt for paranormals was all going to come to nothing anyway.

Though, now that he thought hard about it, some strange things had been happening. Dex doubted there were witches, werewolves, and vampires floating around town. Even so, he wasn't one to just rake in a paycheck for nothing. He didn't want to waste the FBI's money, so he might as well work the real murder case while he was here.

"…. no other tattoos or marks, isn't that correct, Ursula?" Owen's words pulled Dex from his thoughts, and he focused his attention on the crime scene pictures scattered across Owen's desk.

"Nothing. No bruises, and toxicology reports came back clean," Ursula said.

"The victim doesn't seem to have any enemies. I can't find the tattoo parlor that gave her that strange tattoo, but I think that's a dead end anyway," Owen said.

"According to everyone who knew her, Violet was a loner. Kind of shy. Liked to read and didn't party or run with a bad crowd. There doesn't seem to be anyone who would want her dead," DeeDee said.

"Which supports my theory of a serial killer. The voodoo doll is what gets me. It's creepy, and the ties to black magic have me on edge. But the fact that it was left there means the killer is dangerous." Owen glanced at Dex as if seeking confirmation for his theory.

"Sure does. Do you know anyone in town that might be that dangerous?" Dex asked.

Owen shook his head. "No one in town. The people here are good."

Ursula and DeeDee nodded their agreement.

Dex liked the idea that it might be someone from out of town, but it seemed too convenient. It wasn't an assumption he was ready to make just yet. They'd barely started looking into all the clues.

"I think looking into Violet's background is a dead end. We have to focus on the physical evidence," Owen said.

"Like this charm." Dex pointed to one of the photographs, a grainy image of a gold charm with some kind of stone in it. "Did you say you found that in the wound?"

"Yes," Ursula said. "Has to have been from someone that was there during the murder."

"Most likely the killer," Owen said. "Problem is, we haven't been able to find out where the charm was purchased. When we do, we can get a customer list. I have my best guys on it."

"Hopefully it wasn't bought online," DeeDee said.

Owen snapped his fingers. "Good point. I'll have Sanders do an Internet search." He looked up at Dex. "Don't you guys have some fancy image-recognition software we could use for that? You know, that searches the Internet for a match? Maybe you could get us a copy of that."

"I could try." Dex turned to Ursula. "What about physical description? Could you tell from the wound how tall the killer is?"

"Somewhere between five foot four and five foot five. And rather strong. The cleaver was buried deep."

"That's pretty short. Are you sure?" Dex asked.

Ursula nodded.

"Probably someone with one of those inferiority complexes that bulks up their muscles to make up for their height," Owen suggested.

"Okay, so we're waiting to find out more about the charm, what about the murder weapon?" Dex asked.

"No prints. Came from the kitchen at the restaurant."

Dex's brows shot up. "So someone in the kitchen maybe? A coworker dispute?"

"Nope." DeeDee shook her head. "Interviewed everyone, and no disputes. Fact is, the cleaver was one of the extras kept in the back of the kitchen near the doorway that leads to the back hall where the bathrooms are. The kitchen gets pretty busy, and anyone passing back to the bathrooms could have easily grabbed it unseen."

"We're getting a list of folks who were in the restaurant at that time," Owen said before Dex could even suggest it. "That will help, but seems to me we have one clever and dangerous killer on our hands. He probably didn't leave a trail. Maybe he paid cash, or maybe he snuck in the back, but the fact that he left that voodoo doll means he had this all planned out. He's been thinking about this for a long time, and I fear it's only a matter of time before he kills again."

Chapter Fourteen

That night, Issy checked her makeup in the rearview mirror one more time before climbing out of Brown Betty to stand on the sidewalk in front of Les Etoiles. After they'd delivered Raine safely home and tucked her in bed, Ember had insisted on taking Issy to get a juice snack, and well, she'd spilled the beans about her date.

If she'd eaten any of Ember's chocolates, she'd have been mighty suspicious that her cousin had slipped a loose-tongue spell into them, but she hadn't taken a bite. She had no idea what had made her tell Ember she had a date—maybe just because it was better than rehashing what had happened at Enid's over and over again. It certainly wasn't the growing feeling of excitement and swarm of butterflies in her stomach that had made her want to share. She wasn't that excited about having dinner with Dex, and she was determined it wouldn't lead to anything.

Ember, on the other hand, was thrilled and had insisted on helping Issy put on some blush and mascara and a gloss on her lips that was almost gone now from all her nervous biting. She never usually wore makeup at all, but Ember said it would help to enhance her already pretty features. Why in the world she'd let Ember talk her into that, she had no idea. The last thing she wanted was to look attractive to Dex Nolan.

Through the softly glowing light of the front windows, Issy peeked inside and spotted Dex already seated at a small table for two near the back of the bistro. He looked handsome in his black sport coat and burgundy tie. There was something about a man in a suit that got her every time, and her resistance to getting involved with him started to melt like a snowman on a warm spring day.

He'd wanted to pick her up, but Issy had insisted on driving herself. She'd figured it was better to have an escape plan in case things went a little wonky, which they always seemed to do whenever she and Dex were together. Now she was glad. Somehow, she knew that the last thing she needed was for Dex to drive her home after dinner.

Issy closed her eyes and took a deep breath for courage.

This was dinner. Nothing more.

Dinner with the most gorgeous guy she knew, in the most romantic restaurant she'd ever seen, while she did her best to forget the scorching-hot kiss she and said guy had shared.

Why did thoughts of that kiss keep surfacing? She didn't want to think about that. She didn't want to think Dex was handsome. Dex was a human, and there was no way he would understand her magic. As soon as she got close to him, something would happen that would expose her paranormal abilities, and he'd run away in horror. Or worse, arrest her and take her in to be experimented upon in Area 59.

She smoothed her hand down her lavender-colored skirt. The outfit always garnered her a lot of compliments on the rare occasions she wore it. But she hadn't worn it to impress Dex, had she? Maybe she should have worn something less attractive, like a burlap sack, because the way her heart was fluttering, she knew she would have little resistance to Dex Nolan's charms, and if he found her attractive...

But she'd hesitated too long. The maître-d appeared, and before she knew it, she was being escorted over to the table, and she found her mind a whirl of insecure thoughts. What if Dex didn't like purple? What if her strawberry-blond curls clashed with the color? What if—

"Here we are." The maître-d pulled out a chair for Issy.

Dex stood, his hazel eyes warm and his expression stunned, and all her doubts evaporated.

"Hi." He gave her a slow head-to-toe appraisal. "You look... Wow!"

Heat and gratitude prickled up from beneath the scoop neck of her matching lavender twinset. "Thanks."

Issy took her seat then carefully laid her napkin on her lap, looking anywhere but at him, unsure of the strange feelings surging up inside her. She tried to present a calm front. "You clean up pretty good yourself."

"Thanks." He smiled, the crooked one that made her knees wobble. "I don't get to dress up very often in my job."

"Me neither."

A waiter filled their water glasses then took their wine order—white for Issy, red for Dex—before telling them about the specials for the day. Once he'd left, Dex set his menu aside and sat forward, his knees brushing against Issy's beneath the small table.

"I'm so glad you said yes," he said, his tone full of appreciation.

"I'm glad you asked," she replied, surprised to find she meant it. Even though her logical mind was listing off all the reasons why she should run out of the restaurant, the rest of her was firmly planted in the seat and didn't want to leave. All of Issy's earlier nerves had settled, and she could finally take a look around the place and appreciate the décor.

Vintage crystal chandeliers hung from the ceiling, and rich swaths of damask decorated the walls. Candles graced each table along with centerpieces of freshly cut flowers in tasteful shades of white and cream. The whole atmosphere gave a feeling of serenity and security and peace.

Issy smiled across the table at Dex. "I've wanted to come here for ages."

"Pretty nice, isn't it?" He looked around then back at her. "Definitely not my usual kind of place."

"Where do you usually eat?"

"Besides fast food places?" He laughed. "O'Hara's makes a fantastic burger. And, of course, Divine Cravings for dessert."

Issy's eyes narrowed at the mention of Divine Cravings. Had Ember put a charm on one of Dex's desserts? No, she wouldn't do that. It was against witch protocol to charm something without at least one of the parties knowing about it, and Ember had sworn she wouldn't do any such thing.

Issy sat back while the sommelier poured their wine. Luigi had completely wiped Dex's memory of all paranormal-related activity surrounding Christian Vonner's arrest, but she couldn't resist checking for herself to make sure. "Good thing they put that Vonner kid behind bars, huh? After all the weird stuff that happened."

Dex looked at her a moment, blinked, then frowned. "Don't remember anything weird. Pretty open-and-shut case of homicide."

"Yeah." Issy sipped her wine, feeling a rush of relief and regret. Relief because Dex wouldn't haul her off to Area 59 for paranormal experiments by the FBPI. Regret because if he *had* remembered and still asked her out, that meant he'd accepted who she was and what she was and wanted to be with her regardless. Deep inside, Issy knew they could never truly have a relationship together without complete honesty.

Still, even though he had no memory of it, he *had* seen her perform magic that day in the woods, and he'd let her go. He'd even saved her from being taken in by his partner, Stan, and the

FBPI. So maybe there was some hope for them yet.

The waiter returned, and they placed their orders. Filet mignon for him, and roasted salmon for her. He got a salad, and she got soup. The waiter dropped off a basket of freshly baked bread that smelled delicious then left once more.

The alcohol fizzed through Issy's empty stomach. If she wasn't careful, she'd end up like Nikki Pettywood after a day in O'Hara's. She set her glass of wine aside and searched for something to fill the silence and took a roll from the basket. "Back in Silver Hollow, huh?"

"Yep." Dex took a roll too and slathered it with fresh butter. "Seems I'm just in time too. With the new murder and all."

"Oh?" she asked, swallowing hard to avoid choking on her mouthful of bread. "Are you working on that case? I didn't realize the FBI was involved."

"Monitoring it for now, in case local law enforcement asks me to step in and help." He devoured half his food in one bite then shrugged. "I heard you were nearby again this time too. Talk about coincidence."

"Yeah." Issy forced a laugh. "Coincidence."

The waiter brought their first course, and her French onion soup smelled divine, all caramelized onions and melted cheese. She did her best not to dive in headfirst and instead took dainty bites. Dex dug into his salad with gusto, having another roll on the side.

"How's Gordon?" she asked.

"Great." Dex grinned. "Man, I never thought I'd get attached to him so quick, but he's like my best bud. Rides around on my shoulder, waving at everyone. Such a good little guy."

Issy grinned. She'd always known Gordon was special. "You had some questions about his food?"

"Oh yeah. Thanks for reminding me."

They spent the next ten minutes or so discussing the care and feeding of bearded dragons in great detail while they each finished their first course. In fact, Issy was so deep in conversation, she barely noticed when the waiter cleared away their empty plates. "Is he head-bobbing with you?"

"Not that I've noticed," Dex said. "Why?"

"They do that sometimes to show dominance... or for courting."

Dex's brows shot up.

Issy laughed. "If he's not displaying that type of behavior, then I'd say you're safe from unwanted advances and he's pretty content."

"Good." Dex leaned forward and put his forearms on the table. "I want him to be happy."

The more time Issy spent around Dex, the more she liked him. He seemed like a genuinely nice guy, and given that he'd witnessed her performing magic before and let her go, maybe he really wouldn't cut and run when he found out who she really was. Then again, there was the matter of his job with the FBPI. Why would he work there if he were tolerant of paranormals? Clearly, he had no memory of her abilities, or he would have already taken her in... or would he?

Maybe he didn't wish ill will on paranormals like his creepy partner, but if not, why work there? Of course, Dex didn't know that Issy—or anyone in Silver Hollow, for that matter—knew about his *real* job, but maybe she could find out more about his motivations by asking about the job he was pretending he did.

She leaned forward. "Can I ask you something?"

"Go for it."

"What made you decide to work for the small-town-crimes division of the FBI?"

He exhaled slowly and sat back, his happy expression clouding, his eyes turning guarded. "That's a long story."

"I'm sorry." She fiddled with her napkin. Was there really a story, or did he not want to elaborate because he didn't have an appropriate cover story? "I didn't mean to pry."

"No, no. It's fine. I just don't talk about it a lot." He smoothed his tie then took a drink of wine before continuing. "I used to work in high-profile crimes, then I got assigned to a kidnapping case. There was a child involved, and..." He cringed. "Well, the case went sideways, and the child ending up dying."

"Oh, Dex." Without thinking, Issy reached across the table and took his hand, her heart swelling with sympathy. "I'm so sorry."

"Me too." Wincing, he traced his thumb absently over the back of her hand. "I didn't have the heart for kidnapping cases anymore. Not when someone could die. After that day, I vowed I would do everything in my power to protect the innocents under my care." Dex blinked hard then looked up at the ceiling, giving a sad little chuckle. "Truth is, I always thrived on the high-profile action. This job is more... sedate. But I'm finding I kind of like that now."

He didn't release her hand, and she didn't pull away.

A warm tingle started somewhere near Issy's heart and spread outward to her extremities.

He wasn't with the paranormal division because he hated paranormals—he was there for another reason altogether. Maybe this attraction between them could go somewhere after all.

The bell above the door jingled, and in walked Enid Pettywood and Luigi Romano. Enid waved to Issy, and Luigi did his usual stoic chin nod. Funny, she'd never pictured the two of them as friends. Dex seemed to have noticed them too. He hailed the sommelier over for a refill on their wine as the waiter brought their main course. All the while, he watched the newly arrived pair from across the room.

"What do you make of that?" Dex asked Issy, indicating Enid and Luigi.

"Not sure." She concentrated on her food, hoping to distract him. "This looks amazing."

Thankfully, he turned back to his own plate and grinned. "It does, doesn't it?"

Issy dug into her fish, glancing every so often over at Enid and Luigi. They seemed to be deep in discussion, with an occasional smile or laugh thrown into the mix. That was good. If Luigi liked Enid, maybe he wouldn't bring her up on charges to the committee for accidentally summoning a demon—*if* he did figure out it was her. But with any luck, now that the demon was now gone, he wouldn't even dig further into it.

"Taste good?" Dex asked around a mouthful of steak.

"Delicious." The buttery salmon melted in her mouth, and the sautéed summer squash and peppers on the side were the perfect snappy compliment. "How's your steak?"

"Perfect." He finished first then pushed his plate aside. "What are your plans after this?"

Uh-oh. Dangerous territory. Issy figured she'd better make it sound as though she had important business to rush off to. Otherwise, she might end up spending more time with Dex Nolan than she should.

"Go home. Work on some paperwork for the store." She shrugged. "I'm trying to come up with a new marketing slogan for the shop."

"Sounds thrilling." He grinned. "How about a walk?"

"A walk to where?"

"Don't know. I hear they have a really nice riverfront."

"They do." Issy smiled. Her parents had brought her here when she was a child. "Lots of little shops and a lovely boardwalk."

"Sounds great. You wanna check it out?"

Her breath caught at the sparkle in his eyes. She opened her mouth to decline. After all, she had an important marketing slogan to work on. "Sure."

Now where the heck did that come from? She'd meant to say no. To let him down gently. It was almost as if she weren't in control of her own body. Maybe Dex had bewitched her. Issy almost laughed at the thought, but now that she'd agreed, she was glad. She didn't want her time with Dex to end.

After she finished her meal, Dex paid the bill, and they headed down the block toward the river. The night had grown slightly cooler, and Issy couldn't suppress a small shiver.

Dex glanced sideways. "Cold?"

"A little."

"Here." He took off his suit coat and draped it around Issy's shoulders then kept his arm there as well. "That should warm you up."

Warm her up was right. Being surrounded by his heat and scent—sandalwood and vanilla and clean male—it brought all the memories of their kiss rushing back. She stumbled over her feet, and he tucked her tighter into his side.

By the time they reached the boardwalk, Issy felt as though she were floating on air. Dex let his arm slip from around her shoulders and took her hand instead, lacing his fingers through hers. Together, they strolled the riverfront, stopping at booths here and there and enjoying all the twinkling lights and other couples milling about.

They made their way to the end of the boardwalk and stopped at the rail. She peered down at the dark waters below, while Dex leaned back against the railing beside her.

"I've had a really good time tonight, Issy," he said, his voice low and rough.

"Me too." Her toes curled inside her cute purple flats at the deep velvet of his tone. "Thank you for dinner."

Dex looked at her, his hazel eyes so warm and inviting, then leaned in slowly, slowly, giving her plenty of time to pull away if she wanted.

Issy didn't want to pull away. She knew she should. She should run for the hills, but she couldn't help herself. Heck, just one kiss couldn't hurt, could it?

His soft lips brushed hers once, twice, before capturing her mouth.

It was just as she remembered. It was so much better than before.

Issy turned toward him, and her hands slid around his neck while his arms encircled her waist. He tasted of sweet red wine and so many wonderful possibilities. She wanted to stay there forever. She wanted to keep kissing him all night long. She wanted—

A police siren wailed nearby, and they broke apart fast.

Chapter Fifteen

Dex stood for several moments, staring down at Issy.

He hadn't really meant to kiss her tonight, just wanted a chance to get to know her better, maybe see where things might lead for them in the future. Their dinner had been fantastic and the conversation good. In fact, she was one of the few people, outside of the bureau, he'd ever told about why he'd made the shift out of the kidnapping-and-high-profile-crimes division.

The fact that he'd had to lie to her didn't sit right. Then again, he hadn't really lied—he'd just let her believe he was part of the small-town-crimes division instead of the FBPI. But he couldn't very well tell her he was really here seeking paranormals. She'd have laughed him out of the restaurant. And besides, what he'd told her was mostly true—he had every intention of working on the actual crime that had occurred in Silver Hollow.

Her cheeks were flushed, and her eyes had that dreamy look, and if that stupid squad car hadn't pulled up in the alleyway beside them, he would've pulled her right back into his arms and kissed her some more.

An officer got out and ran over to them. "Are you Agent Dex Nolan?"

Dex gave Issy one last long look then turned to the officer. "Yes."

"I need you to come with me."

"What's going on?" Issy asked, her gaze darting between Dex and the policeman, her cheeks growing redder by the second.

The cop glanced around then leaned closer. "The sheriff of Silver Hollow sent me to find you, sir. He says there has been another... *incident.*"

Issy gasped. "Another one?"

"Okay." Dex guided Issy off to the side. "Are you okay getting home, or do you want to ride with me?"

"I can drive myself."

"Okay." Dex walked Issy back to her rusted-out old truck then rushed back to his sedan. Twenty minutes later, he screeched up to the crime scene in Silver Hollow, this one on a slightly busier side street—noticing with slight annoyance that Issy's truck screeched in right behind him.

Dex got out and walked back to her. "I don't think you want to go there. You should go home."

Issy folded her arms across her chest. "I don't take orders from you. This is my town, and I want to see what's going on."

Dex's eyes narrowed. From what he could see, Owen Gleason was bending over a dead body. Odd that Issy always seemed to be around when a dead body was found. But, this time, she'd been with him. He was about to protest again, when she brushed past him and rushed over to Owen.

Well, heck. Guess I better follow.

"What's happened?" Dex knelt beside Owen and took in the details. This victim had a blue rope around her neck, and she was... *alive*! Her chest rose and fell, though her eyes remained closed. "She's not dead?"

"Nope," Owen said. "Not yet, anyway."

Paramedics pushed through the gathering crowd to tend to the victim, and Issy stepped aside to let them in.

Owen held up a voodoo doll triumphantly, the same kind as with the first victim. "Looks like we could have a serial killer on our hands."

Dex frowned, even if his interest was piqued. "People are dying. That's not good."

"True enough." Owen nodded, his eager expression turning grim.

Issy stumbled, and Dex reached for her. "You okay?"

"I just... This shouldn't be happening." She looked scared and confused, and more than anything, Dex wanted to pull her closer and tell her everything would be all right. Before he could, though, her cousins showed up. He remembered meeting them during the Drummond case. There was the gardener—Raine —in her overalls, along with Ember, the chocolatier whose shop he'd been getting those great sea-salted caramels from. And Gray. He owned the local hair salon. Kind of a strange occupation for a guy, at least in Dex's estimation, but to each his own.

All the Quinn cousins exchanged a look that made Dex feel even more like an outsider, a sort of secret communication he wasn't privy to, but he didn't have time to worry about that now. He had one homicide and another attempted killing to solve.

"Wait a minute, let me see that doll," Dex asked the sheriff. It was the same construction as the one found with the dishwasher, but something was off. This one had black stuff dripping from its mouth. He glanced at the blue rope. "Dang!"

"What?" Owen looked concerned. "It's the same kind of doll. I'm sure we got a repeat killer on our hands."

"No, not that," Dex said. "The first doll at the first scene had a blue string around its neck like a noose. And now, tonight, the killer tried to strangle the victim with a blue rope."

Owen glanced toward the ambulance. "Yeah?"

"So the murderer isn't giving us a rendering of their current crime. They're giving us a depiction of the next one."

"Oh..." Owen looked at the evidence bag. "Huh, if that's true, then I bet the next victim will be poisoned."

"Just ducky," Issy said.

Her cousins put their arms around her. Ember leaned closer to peer down at the tiny doll.

Dread bored a hole clean through Dex's stomach as the EMTs closed the back bay doors of the ambulance on the latest victim. There were more similarities Owen hadn't mentioned. It was likely he hadn't caught on to them, but Dex was trained to notice things like this, and the similarities he'd noticed spooked him far more than those crazy voodoo dolls.

All the victims were women.

And they were all redheads.

Issy's strawberry-blond curls glistened beneath the orange streetlights.

If this crazed killer harmed even one precious hair on Issy's head, he would not be responsible for his actions. Dex had failed once to protect those entrusted to his care. This time, he wouldn't screw up again and let Issy or her cousins die because of his lack of diligence.

This time, he'd protect Issy and her family.

No matter the cost.

***

An hour later, Issy was tucked on her living room sofa while Raine fixed them all cups of hot tea in her kitchen. Her cousin seemed to have made a full recovery from her Benadryl-induced coma, which was good. Ember sat on one side of her and Gray on the other. Dex sat in a chair across from her as he watched her carefully.

"I'm sorry." She rubbed her tired eyes. "I still don't understand why you think I'm in danger."

"Because you're a redhead." Dex's tone was filled with patience. "Just like Raine and Ember.

All three of you are at risk. Both of the killer's previous victims had red hair too. I want Owen to put each of you under protective custody until we catch whoever is doing this."

Issy shook her head. The only problem was that the killer wasn't really the killer. Not like Dex thought, anyway. It was the demon inhabiting some unsuspecting host's body. She couldn't tell him that, though, so she went with a more plausible excuse. "The Silver Hollow Police Department is too small to accommodate something like that. Besides, there are plenty of other redheads in town. I don't need protection."

She was a witch, and now more the ever, she knew she had confidence in her abilities. If it came down to a paranormal battle, she could more than hold her own. She'd proved that with Christian Vonner and all his vile, dark deeds. If she was strong enough to defeat him, she was strong enough to defeat anything or anyone.

"I disagree." Dex pushed to his feet and paced her tiny living room.

Issy had no idea why he'd gone all caveman protective, but she didn't like it. Not one bit. Sure, the kiss they'd shared back on the boardwalk had been spectacular, and yes, the time they'd spent together prior had been pretty magical too. But it didn't make him the boss of her. And his current alpha-male mood didn't bode well for when she told him the truth about her abilities.

Nope. Perhaps things between them wouldn't work out after all.

Perhaps it was best that that kiss hadn't progressed to something more.

No matter how much it hurt to realize it.

"I need to check in with Owen at the station." Dex stalked toward the door, stopping to face her one last time. "Tonight was nice."

Part of her wanted to run after him and tell him that this evening had been way more than nice. But the other part of her knew she couldn't. With the way he was acting, she was starting to remember why she'd thought things would never work between them. Besides, now she had to deal with the fact that the demon was still around and figure out how to get rid of it. Issy lowered her head and said, "See you later, Dex."

"See you, Issy."

After he'd gone, Issy couldn't forget the look on his face as he'd walked out her door—hurt, crushed, defeated.

"Dang it, the potion didn't work!" Ember said as soon as they heard Dex's car drive off.

"At least now we know what the similarity the demon wants is, but if having red hair is the common theme, then all three of us Quinn girls need to take extra precautions." Raine took up residence in Dex's now vacant seat, her face dead serious. Issy's heart constricted. She wondered if Raine was having doubts about being able to protect herself with her magical abilities. Issy knew how that felt—she'd had those same doubts once herself.

Ember shrugged. "Maybe Dex was right. Maybe we should let Owen help protect us."

"Owen's got his hands full with the case," Gray said. "We take care of our own."

Issy sighed and squared her shoulders. "Gray's right. We need to handle this ourselves. Did you guys see Nikki doing anything suspicious tonight?"

"Nope." Gray raked a hand through his black hair. "Not a thing."

"I'm beginning to think Nikki's not possessed at all," Ember said.

"Great." Issy pinched the bridge of her nose between her thumb and forefinger. Ember might have just been defending her potion-making skills, but the thing was, she'd felt the same way when they'd last seen Nikki, but maybe the demon was just a good actor. "Well, if Nikki didn't attack that woman tonight, then who did?"

Chapter Sixteen

"That's a good question." Raine sipped her tea and stared at the front door. "Maybe you should go after him."

"Why would I go after him?" Issy crossed her arms against the ache in her chest. So she'd just had the best date of her life. Didn't mean she had to go crazy over the guy. "We've got important things to discuss. And why don't you tease Gray about Starla for a while and forget about me and Mr. Paranormal Hunter, huh? The way Gray was drooling all over the floor of her shop earlier, I should've brought a bucket."

Ember's emerald-green eyes widened, and Raine snorted. They both looked at Gray. "You've got the hots for a Knight."

"I don't have the hots for anybody," Gray said, his tone testy. Dots of crimson dotted his high cheekbones. "And I wasn't drooling. She must have hexed me. Can we get down to business here, please?"

"Whatever." Raine went back into the kitchen to fix herself another cup of tea. When she returned, she had Mortimer's pot tucked under one arm. The poor guy looked a bit wilted, which was unusual. Normally, plants thrived around Raine. "Hey, Issy," she said. "Think you can keep Morty here for a couple of days? He's a bit under the weather, and spending time with you and Bella always seems to revive him."

"Sure. I'm happy to keep Morty whenever you need me to. You know that."

"Thanks." Raine sat Morty's pot on the coffee table in front of her then sank back into her seat and curled her legs beneath her. Bella trotted over to sniff the plant. She must have sensed that he wasn't well, because as soon as she got near she backed up a bit and looked at Issy uncertainly.

"It's okay. Morty's not well. You can cheer him up."

"*Yip!*"

A warning vibe tingled at Issy, and she smiled down at the little Pom. How cute. Bella was warning her away from the ailing plant. "It's okay. He can't make us sick."

Bella backed away from the plant and jumped into Issy's lap.

"She's coming along pretty good," Ember said.

Issy nodded proudly. "She is. Too bad that doesn't help us with the demon. Obviously, our little exorcism the other day at Enid's place didn't work, and it's still around."

"True," Ember said, setting her tea aside. "But, really, I don't think Nikki's the person it's inhabiting. Remember how I said me and Gray would tail her?"

"Yep," Issy said.

"No." Raine frowned.

"You were asleep," Ember said to Raine. "Gray and I watched her the entire time, right up until Owen found the second victim, and she didn't go anywhere near the scene of the crime. So how could she have tried to strangle the victim?"

"Demons can move at super-speed, but maybe that explains why she didn't finish the job. Maybe she knew you were watching her and didn't have time?" Issy suggested. She knew it was a lame reason, but she couldn't think of anything else.

The others gave her the side-eye, and she shrugged. "It was just an idea."

"Now that you mention it, it is kind of odd that the demon hesitated to kill this last person," Ember said.

"Maybe it has a conscience," Gray suggested.

"Either way, we're back to square one with finding out who the demon's host is." Issy shook her head. "And I know one other person who would definitely have that charm. Starla."

"Yeah, and she has been acting funny," Raine said. "With coming to our end of town and contacting Gray and all."

"She was trying to help." Gray ran his hands through his hair. "I mean, that's what she said. Honestly, she didn't seem possessed..."

"Demons can be good actors. Maybe she told you Nikki bought the charm to try to cast suspicion away from her and frame Nikki," Ember said.

"I don't know." Gray sounded dubious. "If that was the case, then why was there a big electrical disturbance when you fed the potion to Nikki?"

"Good question."

"How potent was the stuff you put in those chocolates?" Gray asked.

"Potent enough," Ember said. "It's possible that the demon jumped from Nikki into the electrical system when we fed her the candy. Because Enid ate some of it too, there probably wasn't enough of the potion in Nikki's system to banish it completely and send it back where it came from. Then it traveled through the wires and somehow found another host."

"There weren't any electrical disturbances in town, so it must have found someone fast," Gray said.

"Would the next host have to be in close proximity?" Issy asked. "It might help us to figure out who the next host might be."

"I'm not sure," Ember said. "I think it can travel rapidly, though, through the electrical circuits. I mean, electricity is pretty much instant."

"Oh man." Gray scrubbed a hand over his face. "If that's the case, then it could've gone anywhere and gotten into anyone."

"Not just anyone," Issy said. "The same rules still apply. The host would have to be someone weak enough or sick enough to accept it. Still, it seems pretty impossible we'll find it in time. There's only three days left until the new moon."

Her shoulders slumped as Issy looked from Ember to Raine then back again. "If the killer is targeting redheads, whoever's doing this will need to step up their game. With the last victim still alive, they'll need a new sacrifice."

"There is one more clue." Ember cuddled Endora and Bellatrix under her chin. "The doll at the crime scene. According to what it depicted, the next murder will be a poisoning."

"That doesn't really help us much." Gray sighed. "There are a million ways to poison someone."

"True." Ember smiled at him over the top of a kitten head. "But those weren't black drops dripping from the doll's mouth."

"They weren't?" Raine asked, leaning forward.

"Nope." Ember placed her kittens back in their basket then straightened her skirt. "I took a closer look before Owen bagged the evidence. They were tiny mushrooms."

A spark of hope reignited inside Issy. "There's only one place in Silver Hollow to get decent mushrooms for potions, spell casting, and poisoning."

"The secret field," Gray said.

"Yep." Ember grinned.

"Perfect!" Issy pushed to her feet, her energy renewed along with her optimism. "All we have to do is catch the killer digging them up, and we'll know who the new host is."

Chapter Seventeen

The next afternoon, Issy drove old Brown Betty around to Divine Cravings to pick up Ember. They were headed out to the mushroom field to keep watch so Gray, who'd been there all morning, could get back to work. Ember all but skipped out of her store and climbed into the passenger seat then waved to her assistant behind the counter. "Hey," she said as she buckled her seat belt. "Lovely day."

"It is." Issy glanced at Ember, wondering how her cousin could be so chipper when a murderous demon was on the loose. "Though I can't help but feel like a black cloud is hovering over us with this demon thing going on."

Ember's cheery expression darkened. "Yeah, me too. Do you think we might be in danger?"

"If the demon's looking for redheads, we might be." Issy gnawed her bottom lip. "Are you worried about fighting a demon?"

"I think we could take one. *If* we were together. They fight dirty, though, and use all kinds of energy tricks that we're not equipped to handle. Especially alone, attempting that might result in full energy depletion." Ember's face turned grim, and Issy shuddered at the thought. It took tremendous amounts of energy to cast spells, and if one overdid it, one could drain their entire energy source. And full energy depletion usually resulted in death.

"Well, then, I guess we better stick together." Issy signaled and pulled out into traffic then did a double take in her rearview mirror. Dex Nolan was right behind her, in his vintage sedan. "Um, quick change of plans."

She signaled and made a quick right then another quick left before pulling off to the side of the road on a residential street and crouching down in her seat.

Ember gripped the dashboard and gave her a concerned look. "Everything okay?"

"Dex was behind us," Issy whispered, gesturing for Ember to get down too. "I don't want him to follow us to the mushroom field."

"You remember it's enchanted, right?" Ember gave her cousin some serious side-eye. "Humans can't see it."

"I know, but we don't need him following us into the woods and then seeing us disappear." Issy leaned up a bit to peer out the windshield then ducked down quickly again at the sound of an approaching car. She was being ridiculous. It was just that after that wonderful date last night and then that mind-blowing kiss, Dex Nolan had her on edge.

Of course, the fact that Bella was dancing around her feet as though she had ants in her tiny pants and was telepathing strange signals to her didn't help either. Issy gave her familiar a concerned look. "What is it, Bella? Huh? I know, Mommy's acting strange."

"Got that right," Ember said then twisted around to look out the back window. "He's gone. We better hurry, 'cause Gray's already left the field. Don't want to leave it unattended for too long."

Issy scooted up in her seat, moved Bella to safety in the back, and then restarted the old truck's engine and pulled out into the road again. They reached the outskirts of Silver Hollow and made a left turn down an all but invisible path into the woods surrounding the town.

The farther they drove, the darker it got, until only a few hazy beams of dappled sunlight streamed through the heavy forest canopy. The air here was cooler and smelled of musty, rotted leaves and dirt. Issy eased the truck around a bend and down into a little valley near a bubbling brook. She parked off to the side of the dirt path, and she and Ember got out.

Bella immediately sniffed all of the trees within a five-foot radius while Bellatrix and Endora peeked out from the top of the tote bag Ember had them in as the cousins walked the short distance to the stream and surveyed the area.

A few yards from where they were stood a shadowed figure. Issy nudged her cousin in the arm and pointed. "Someone's here."

The figure was bent over and appeared to be digging in the dirt.

Issy swallowed hard around the lump of tension in her throat. "Let's go."

As they got closer, however, her heart sank. It was Enid and Becky. The little porker was snuffling the ground and pawing the soil as if helping Enid dig.

Bella tugged on her leash, eager to say hello. Issy followed behind her, guessing this must've been what her little familiar was so excited about in the truck. Bella and Becky were true pals.

Enid stood in the nonpoisonous, gourmet section of the field and clearly had no clue of the imminent danger. Issy cleared her throat, hoping not to startle the older lady. "Hi, Enid."

"Oh!" Enid whirled around fast, and Becky oinked. "Issy, dear. You scared me. I didn't see anyone else arrive."

"We parked a little way down." Issy glanced at Ember then back to the elderly witch. "What are you doing here, Enid?"

"Searching for some rare Trabucco mushrooms. They're one of the special ingredients in my secret pizza sauce recipe I promised to Luigi." She held up the small bundle in her hand and opened it so Issy could peer inside. "Of course, I'm not going to give him the location of our mushroom field, so I came out here to dig a few up myself. Thought it would be a nice gesture to give him some of the actual mushrooms to get him started on his first batch of sauce. I know he's from the committee and all, but it would be smart for us to make friends with him, don't you think?"

"Yes, that's smart." Issy wrapped an arm around the smaller woman's shoulders. For a minute there, Issy had been worried Enid was out here digging up poisonous mushrooms. But Enid couldn't be possessed by the demon, because she'd eaten Ember's candy, and besides, she didn't have any poisonous mushrooms, only the Trabuccos.

"He's not so bad, you know," Enid said. "Luigi, I mean. He's really kind of a pussycat underneath. A tortured soul."

Tortured soul that wants to bring the punishment hammer down on whoever unleashed the demon. Issy didn't voice her thoughts, though. The more Enid helped him, the more he'd like her, and hopefully, that would go in her favor if she was brought before the committee. Plus, the previous conversation with him had left Issy doubting if he actually was even interested in turning anyone in.

"Well, Ember and I are going to head across the stream for a moment. We'll see you later."

"Be careful," Enid called from behind them. "Those are the bad kind."

Issy waved then followed Ember across a tiny footbridge to the poisonous side of the field. Here, the light was downright gloomy. There was no birdsong, no breeze rustling the leaves, just ominous silence and the smell of danger. Issy picked up Bella and held her in her arms, not wanting to take the chance of her tiny dog getting sick from being near the poisonous plants.

"The black mushrooms are on the hill over there." Ember pointed toward a large tree, its dead limbs twisting up into the air. They started toward it slowly. Over here on the poisonous side, it was as if the air were thicker, harder to breathe. And time seemed to slow, almost as if the area itself were cautioning them to think about what they were doing and take their time. Poisonous mushrooms were a serious matter.

Ember crested the hill first then stood looking at the ground, her mouth in a tight line. "Oh dear. This isn't good."

"What's wrong?" Issy moved in beside her cousin, her stomach sinking as they peered down at the freshly dug holes in the earth. "Someone's been here already."

"They've already dug up the mushrooms." Ember sighed.

Bella whined, and Issy hugged her close. The poor little thing was trembling. Maybe she was cold. It was pretty dismal in this small patch of woods. Issy and Ember started back the way they'd come, Issy's steps slow with defeat. "They must have come after Gray left and before we got here. Which means we'll have to find another way to catch our killer."

Chapter Eighteen

Dex sat in his Buick along the side of the two-lane highway, Gordon perched on the back of the seat next to him. He'd tailed Issy and her cousin to the woods, but for some weird reason when he'd gone to turn off the road, the path they'd followed wasn't there. He'd backtracked two or three times but couldn't find it. So he'd finally given up and decided to wait instead.

He glanced over at Gordon, who looked back at him with the lizard equivalent of a "What's up, dude?" expression. "I know, buddy." Dex sighed. "Pretty pathetic, huh?"

Gordon rose on his hind legs and lifted his front paw as if in agreement.

Yep. Nothing like camping out in the middle of nowhere to protect a woman who wanted nothing to do with him or his guardianship. Still, he'd vowed to watch over her and her nutty family, and that was exactly what he intended to do, whether Issy liked it or not.

What the heck could they be doing in there anyway? He checked his watch for the umpteenth time then shook his head. It had been over a half an hour already. He'd figured maybe they were walking their pets or something. It was a nice day out, and he seemed to remember Issy mentioning her love of the outdoors back when he was working the Drummond case.

The Drummond case. Dex frowned. Every time he remembered those days, something didn't sit right inside him, like a wrong puzzle piece jammed into place. There was something about being in the woods with Issy, something about that killer they'd caught here, something he and Issy had shared...

Scowling, he shook off the hazy thoughts. It seemed that no matter how hard he concentrated, all he ever got was a splitting headache for his trouble.

His phone dinged. Stan again. Dex debated not taking it, but he was afraid Stan would just hop on the next plane out if he thought there were paranormal activities. Better to be able to talk him out of coming in the first place.

"Stan! How's the case going?" Dex tried to sound as though he were happy to hear from him.

"Good. Wrapping things up soon. I heard some strange rumblings about dark magic going on in Silver Hollow. What's going on down there?"

"Yeah, I'm on that. Unfortunately, I don't think it has anything to do with the paranormal." Dex tried to sound disappointed.

"No? Why not?" Stan really did sound disappointed.

"Well, you heard about the murder the other day."

"The dishwasher dumpster murder?"

"Yeah, that one. Anyway, there was a doll found with the body."

"A voodoo doll. Black magic." Stan's voice rose with excitement.

"Seemed that way at first, but there was an attempted second murder, and turns out the dolls aren't voodoo dolls. They're clues to the next murder. So I'm afraid we just have an average run-of-the-mill serial killer on our hands."

"Oh no. Really? What about the energy disruptions—that happens when there's magic."

"I told you that was just a bad transformer. Haven't been any since."

"Oh, right. Dang. I was hoping we could get someone really powerful from Silver Hollow. I know there's magic there. I can feel it."

Dex's chest constricted at the vengeance in Stan's words. The guy really wanted to experiment on a paranormal. A few weeks ago, Dex might have thought it was funny because there was no such thing, but given recent events, he was starting to question his earlier beliefs. Something was off with this dishwasher killing, but Dex didn't know if it actually pointed to anything magic.

Whether it did or not, he sure as heck didn't want Stan down here trying to drag people back to Area 59. Dex was starting to get attached to Silver Hollow and its residents, especially one in particular, and the farther away Stan was from them, the better.

"Sorry, buddy. Nothing paranormal here. At least not with this case. I'll stick on it, though, and let you know."

"Roger. I'll have my bags ready."

Stan clicked off, and Dex took a deep breath. He didn't know how long he'd be able to hold Stan off from coming here. Good thing he was tied up in that other case. As soon as it was over, though, he'd be wanting to come to Silver Hollow, and Dex had better be ready. He had the feeling he might need to protect the residents from more than just the serial killer that was on the loose now. He might be protecting them from his own partner.

Dex thumbed through his messages. A new one appeared from Owen. The sheriff had found some new information on the case.

After tossing the phone back on the seat, Dex secured Gordon's leash to the seat belt then started his engine. Time to head back to the station. Didn't look as if anything much was going to happen here.

A few minutes later, he pulled into the small parking lot in front of the Silver Hollow Police headquarters and unhooked Gordon, giving him time to scramble up on his shoulder before exiting the vehicle.

Owen met him by the desk of Myra Bell, the station receptionist.

"I've tracked down the charm found in the wound of the first victim." Owen led Dex through a doorway leading to the back area and the sheriff's office. On his desk, in a small baggie, sat the evidence in question.

Dex had only seen the charm in a grainy photo before, and he leaned over the bag and squinted. "Why are there puncture marks in the top of the bag? Looks like something chewed it."

"No idea. Defective, maybe?" Owen shrugged. "Came into police custody that way."

"Huh." Dex leaned down so Gordon could climb off his shoulder and onto Owen's desk. "Do you mind?"

"Not at all." Owen cooed to a waving Gordon. "Cute little guy, isn't he?"

"He's my main man," Dex said. "What else have you found?"

"That charm came from a store on the south side of Silver Hollow named Charmed. Went there yesterday and questioned the owner, gal named Starla Knight. She said she sold two of those charms, one to Nikki Pettywood and another to a tourist. Some young guy who paid cash so the wife wouldn't see it on the credit card bill." He handed Dex the customer records. "Of course, I went to question Nikki right away."

"What'd she say?" Dex glanced at the list. He saw Nikki's name and address but only the first name for the tourist and the words "paid in cash." He set the list aside, out of Gordon's chewing range, and gave him a treat from his pocket instead to keep the lizard occupied.

"Nikki said she bought the charm as a gift for her grandmother, Enid, and that it's on her grandmother's bracelet right now."

"Is it?"

"Don't know. Went to speak with Enid this morning but couldn't find her."

180

"Hmm." Dex took a deep breath. "Seems a long shot she'd be the killer. Enid's too old and frail. It takes a lot of muscle to bury a meat cleaver into someone's back."

"True enough." Owen narrowed his gaze. He'd always reminded Dex of that actor, the shaggy blond one from *Zoolander*. "Then that leaves the tourist. Which would make me feel a whole lot better, knowing it isn't one of our own. Then again, seems like he's hanging around to kill more people, so maybe I don't feel so good."

"Yeah, that part's not good. But I don't think Enid would have the strength." *Would she?* Dex remembered seeing her tug that pig along when it wanted to go in one direction and she in another. She was pretty strong, and hadn't Ursula said the killer was around five foot four or five? By Dex's estimation, that was about how tall the old lady was.

Owen made a face. "Funny thing is, there were several witnesses who swore they saw Enid in the diner right before the dishwasher's body was discovered, which puts her there at the time of the murder. All seems like too much of a coincidence to me."

"The worst thing we can do is jump to conclusions." Dex knew that from personal experience with the kidnapping case. "Let's find out where Enid was when you found victim number two then go from there. How is the victim, by the way?"

"She'll pull through," Owen said. "She's awake now and talking, though her voice is pretty rough from damage to her windpipe. Docs say she should make a full recovery, though, which is good."

"Good." Dex stroked a finger down Gordon's back. "Does she remember anything about what happened last night?"

"Not much. Didn't see her assailant." Owen took a seat behind his desk. "She states she was attacked from behind. Odd thing, though. She said it was almost like her assailant was battling with themselves. Said they kept arguing with themselves while they were choking her, fighting about whether they were going to finish her off or not. Like they had a split personality."

"That is weird. Did you get any specifics on the voice? Gender? Age?" Dex felt a surge of excitement. An old lady like Enid would have a much different voice from the young tourist guy. This could help narrow things down.

Owen shook his head. "Nope. The assailant whispered."

"Oh." Dex's excitement evaporated. It was nearly impossible to tell gender or age from a whisper. And with the victim preoccupied with being strangled, Dex figured they weren't exactly concentrating on the depth or inflection of the whisper.

"The victim thinks that's why she survived. The self-arguing, I mean. The killer didn't wait around long enough to be sure she was dead."

Dex had dealt with his fair share of murderers when he'd worked on the FBI side of the bureau, and they always made sure their victims didn't live to tell any tales. Unfortunately, that didn't help poor Enid. In fact, all the arguing and bumbling only pointed to the fact that this was probably a first-timer. Still, it was hard to picture good-natured, absent-minded Enid offing anyone. She'd have to be either super clever to totter around town hiding all that strength, or super cold blooded to kill her first victim then proceed to have lunch right afterward.

Either way, it made Dex shudder.

Chapter Nineteen

That night after work, the Quinn cousins all met up at The Main Squeeze to discuss their investigation. Issy sipped on another Pineapple Express, swearing the things were addictive. "The killer's got the mushrooms."

"I can't believe they got there in those few minutes after I left." Gray shook his head, staring down into his Pomegranate Passion. It seemed that the drink was still on special, at least according to Karen's menu board.

"Did you see anyone on your way out?" Issy asked.

"Nope, and there were no dig marks when I was there, either," Gray said.

"What about Enid?" Ember asked. "Did you see her? Maybe she ran over and dug them up after you left then ran back to the other side when we came."

"I saw her with Becky when I was leaving, but she was way over in the other field." Gray pressed his lips together. "She doesn't move very fast. I don't see how she could have dug those up so quickly."

"And besides, she only had the Trabucco mushrooms when we saw her," Issy pointed out. "Not to mention that she ate the candies with the potion, so the demon couldn't be in her. Could it?"

"Doubtful." Gray sighed. "They must have timed it perfectly. Almost like whoever it was is privy to our plans."

"Yeah, right." Raine chuckled then sipped some awful-looking brown concoction Karen had touted as "super healthy." Kale and bean curd and guava and... Issy gagged just thinking about it.

Bella must have felt the same way, because she let out a soft growl as she watched Raine drink the thing. Issy rubbed her behind the ears, and the dog calmed. "New moon's in two days."

"According to my research, the demon needs to send three redheads over by the new moon if it wants permanent residence in its current body," Ember said. She had a Pineapple Express, same as Issy. "It needs two more since it botched the last job, so now it'll be looking to speed things up with this new victim."

"At least we have three eligible redheads right here for it to choose from," Raine said.

"Are you thinking we can set up a trap?" Gray asked.

"We could." Issy nodded. "Tonight."

DeeDee swerved to the curb in her squad car. "Hey, Quinn cousins. How's it going?"

"Good," they all said in unison.

DeeDee pulled up a chair to their table then lowered her voice. "I stopped by to let you know Owen found out that charm came from Starla's shop. He also knows she sold it to Nikki. And Nikki said she bought it for Enid."

"What?" Ember's voice rose in alarm. "Enid would never kill anyone. Neither would Nikki."

"No, but the demon possessing her would." DeeDee leaned closer. "Besides, everyone knows demons lie like crazy. If Nikki is hosting a demon, chances are good it was doing the talking when Owen questioned her. Chances are also good it would've stolen that charm off Enid's bracelet and planted it at the crime scene just to focus attention away from itself."

"We know the demon's not in Nikki's body anymore." Ember told DeeDee about what happened at their visit to Enid's house the day before and the potion-infused chocolates and how she and Gray had been watching Nikki when the second victim was strangled.

"There's still a chance it will continue to want Enid blamed for the murders, though," DeeDee said. "Why not deflect attention away from its new host until it kills its quota of redheads?"

"Makes sense," Raine said then drained her cup of icky juice. "I have a great idea. If the killer is trying to frame Enid, then it is likely keeping a close eye on her, so why don't we give it the perfect opportunity it can't refuse? All three of us go to Enid's cottage tonight. That's three redheads for the price of one, right?"

"I don't know," Gray said. "Sounds pretty dangerous. Maybe you all should wait until I can come too."

"We can take care of ourselves," Issy said. "Besides, if you're lurking around, the demon might get spooked and not reveal itself. Better if you stay behind. We'll call if we need help."

"Sounds like a plan, ladies." Raine sat back and grinned.

"Yep." Ember stood and smoothed the front of her dress. "I need to run back to my place and drop off the kittens. Wouldn't want them to get hurt."

"I'll drop off Bella at my house too." Issy pushed to her feet as well. "Plus, I think Dex might be following me. I'll lose his tail and meet you guys at Enid's after sundown."

Chapter Twenty

Around eight p.m., Issy pulled up half a block down from Enid's and got out of her truck. She'd been right. Dex had tried to tail her again, but she'd lost him down some old back roads. Living in Silver Hollow all her life gave her certain advantages when it came to quick getaways.

Still, she was sure he'd find her again sooner or later, so she put a quick vanishing charm on Brown Betty then hurried down the sidewalk. Honestly, if they weren't in the middle of trying to locate this stupid demon and vanquish it, she might find his concern endearing. But, right now, his meddling was only a major pain in her butt. Humans had no business nosing around in paranormal affairs.

They cleaned up their own messes. End of story.

Besides, Dex could get hurt in a magical fight, and then she'd never forgive herself.

Her cousins' cars were there, but they weren't outside. Issy glanced at Enid's, a strange feeling of foreboding gathering like storm clouds inside her.

"Good thing I caught you. You need to be careful."

Issy whirled around to see Brimstone trotting up from behind her. His sleek charcoal fur gleamed black in the shadows cast from the streetlight. He looked ruffled. She leaned down and picked a long hair off his side. Orange tabby. "What do you mean?"

"You know how it is with demons." Brimstone's golden-orange eyes glanced toward Enid's house nervously. He seemed hesitant and unsure of himself. Not like his normal demeanor at all. "You can't trust them."

Issy held up the hair. "Or their cats?"

"What? No. That's from Divinity, the cat at Charmed."

"Right. Seems like you're spending an awful lot of time with her." What was making Brimstone act so strangely? It almost reminded her of the way Gray had acted when they were in Charmed. Had Divinity put a hex on Brimstone, as they'd thought Starla had done to Gray?

Thoughts of Starla made her wonder. Starla had access to the same charms that were found on the body. Starla had been acting strange, and she had appeared downtown right after Issy had cast the finding spell for the charms. Her offer to help them was out of character, but not if she wanted to feed them information to set someone else up.

Starla had told Owen she'd sold the charm to Nikki, and Issy guessed that part was true. What if Nikki really *had* bought a charm and told Starla it was for Enid? The charms were distinct, and according to Starla's record of only two customers, she didn't sell them often, so the demon could easily have framed Enid by dropping the same exact charm into the wound. But then Enid would still be able to produce her charm to prove her innocence. Unless the demon planned to grab the charm from Enid's bracelet at some point.

Then something Brimstone had said earlier chilled her blood. He'd said he'd seen Nikki passed out behind O'Hara's Tuesday afternoon and he'd smelled sage burgers. Issy had thought that was a strange combination for a burger. Sage went better with chicken. But now she realized that the sage he'd smelled must have been from Raine burning it behind the diner to vanquish the demon. But if Nikki had been passed out behind O'Hara's, how could she have killed Violet? The medical examiner had said that Violet was killed only moments before she was discovered, at the same time Nikki was lying passed out in the alley.

Oh crap. What if the demon had been possessing Starla all this time and was never in Nikki at all?

"Spit it out, Brimstone. Are you saying you know who the demon is?"

His eyes narrowed. "Not for sure. I don't want to say in case I'm wrong. But if I'm right, you're gonna be blown away. I just wanted to make sure you were extra careful, especially tonight."

What was with all this hedging? Brimstone was up to something. Or had been put up to something by someone... or someone's cat.

She didn't have time for this nonsense. "Listen, if you know something, you better spit it out. Let me help. The demon's name begins with an 'S,' and she owns a jewelry store." Issy looked around for Starla's car. What did she drive, anyway? Was she here, inside Enid's right now?

A hollow feeling blossomed in Issy's chest. If the demon was already at Enid's and Raine and Ember—the two redheads it needed to complete the sacrifice—were inside, they could be in trouble!

"Huh? It's not—"

But Issy didn't even hear Brimstone. She was already sprinting to Enid's door.

Issy ripped the door open and barged into the living room, her glance darting around in search of Starla.

"Oh, thank goodness you're here." Enid stood on one side of the room, her face pale. She pointed a shaky finger toward the dining room, where Issy spotted what looked like a pizza on the table and Ember on the floor, out cold.

"Oh no!" Issy rushed to her cousin's side. "Enid, please. Tell me what's going on."

"I'm not sure, dear. Ember said something about the pizza... Apparently, it's from Luigi's oven, the same sauce recipe I gave him. Anyway, she and Raine started to argue, then there was a whoosh of air, and Ember stumbled then fell to the floor. I tried to help her, but I'm afraid my spell must have gotten messed up again. You know how that happens when I'm flustered. Instead of helping her up, it put her out like a light..."

Enid waved her arm around the scene, her gold charm bracelet glittering beneath the dining room lights.

"Where's Starla?"

Enid froze in place, her hand wavering in the air. "Starla? You mean Starla Knight? Why would she be here?"

The charms dangling from Enid's bracelet caught Issy's eye. They were gold and enamel like the ones from Charmed, but it wasn't necessarily any of the charms on the bracelet that had her worried. It was the one empty loop where a charm *should* have been.

Raine stepped in beside Issy and shook her head. "We weren't fighting, Enid."

Mind racing, Issy checked her unconscious cousin's pulse and breathing. Both were a bit fast but still present.

Issy's stomach sank. If Starla had been here, Raine would have let on. But she hadn't said a thing, though Issy sensed something off about her. Was she trying to warn Issy somehow? But why? If Starla wasn't there, there was no reason to worry.

Then it hit her. The demon wasn't Starla or Nikki after all. And they'd fallen right into its trap.

Why hadn't she figured it out sooner?

All the clues thus far were pointing toward Enid being the killer. She'd been in the diner when the first victim was found. She'd also been downtown when Issy cast the spell calling the charms to the area, but since Enid had already been there before she'd cast the spell, she hadn't even considered her. And she'd been the only person they'd seen in the mushroom field.

Mushrooms...

Issy glanced at the pizza still sitting on the table, one half-eaten slice lying where Ember had sat. And, underneath the box, she saw the twig arm of a voodoo doll. If she wasn't mistaken, there were two more lying beside it. "Where were you last night, Enid?"

"What, dear?" The elderly witch looked taken aback. "Why would you ask me that? We need to help poor Ember. If I remember correctly, I seem to have—"

"Don't play dumb." Issy straightened and sidled toward Raine, remembering her earlier conversation with Ember. If they combined their powers, they might be able to defeat the demon, and since Ember was out cold, it was up to just her and Raine. "I know what you're up to."

"Whatever do you mean, dear?" Enid's expression grew more perplexed. "Honestly, you young people get me so flustered."

Issy sighed. This demon was apparently a fine actor too. "Seriously, cut the act. I'm talking to the demon inside Enid now. You must have possessed her that day at tea when Ember brought over the chocolates. I bet you jumped out of Nikki when she ate those potion-infused maple creams. It actually makes sense, demon. Jumping from Nikki to someone close by. Especially Enid, since she's older and frail. Easy pickings for a demon to possess. And now that I recall, Enid had indigestion and was confused."

"What? You think I'm possessed by the demon? Don't be ridiculous. You know I couldn't have tried to strangle the last person. I was on the other side of town. You saw me in the restaurant, remember?"

Issy frowned. She had seen Enid when she'd been with Dex. She wouldn't have had time to be strangling someone in Silver Hollow. And if the demon was inside Enid, why was it standing there talking to her and not taking action? "But the only other people that were there the day we brought the candies with the potion..."

A funny feeling niggled at the pit of Issy's stomach as she thought back to that afternoon.

Enid hadn't been the only frail one there the day they'd tried to vanquish that demon.

She glanced over at Raine. The scratches on her arms were crusting and oozing. Her face took on a demonic tint, turning her peaches-and-cream complexion to a sickly gray. Her peridot-green eyes were nothing but dark, soulless holes.

Raine laughed, but not her usual pleasant laugh. This one was deep from the bowels of hell. "That's right, cuz, you figured it out... the demon wasn't in Enid. I'm right here!"

Chapter Twenty-One

Faster than a lightning strike, Raine grabbed a nearby lamp from a side table and tore off the shade, pointing the bulb at Issy. Piercing red flames glowed in her eyes as she aimed and shot forth white-hot bolts of electricity.

Issy screamed and huddled against the wall to avoid the flying shards of glass from the shattering bulb. Then she launched herself at Raine, determined to wrestle the demon out of her cousin with her own two hands if necessary. They tumbled across the floor. Issy grabbed the nearby discarded shade and hurled it at Raine's head, hoping to knock her out. Raine grabbed a porcelain figurine of a frog and whacked Issy hard on the shoulder in an attempt to dislodge her, but she wasn't letting go. There was too much at stake.

Over and over, they rolled across the floor in a tangle of limbs and red hair, ramming into furniture and knocking it askew. Issy did her best to keep Raine's hands locked at her sides, but every so often, one would get free, and bolts of rogue electricity would sizzle through the air.

"I was never in Nikki, by the way," the demon snarled. It seemed that it was also talkative. Just her luck. "I started out in Enid, then she ate those tainted candies, and I had to jump to a new host. Your beloved cousin here had all those lovely scratches, giving me a perfect entry point."

Issy screeched in outrage. They rolled the other way across the living room floor, whamming into the sofa and pushing it halfway into the kitchen. "Get. Out. Of. My. Cousin's. Body!"

"No!" the demon roared. "This is all your fault. You had to go and figure this all out and screw everything up. You couldn't just mind your own business. You stuck your nose in where it didn't belong. If you hadn't, I could've just fed you and Ember poisoned pizza, and the sacrifices would've been done. I could've framed Enid then stayed in this realm, this host, forever. But no!"

"Wait!" Issy was desperate to distract it so she could come up with a plan. "Why redheads? And why make the dolls?"

"Why not redheads? The rules only say the victims need to have something in common. The dolls were just to keep myself occupied and to show how clever I am and how stupid you are."

"Well, you weren't that clever. We did figure out about the mushrooms."

"But you never figured out whose body I was really in!" The demon wrenched free of Issy's grip. Sparks showered through the living room. Burn marks scarred the walls, ceiling, and floor. Even Issy's hair was singed, but still she fought.

No way would this demon take Raine. No. Way.

"Now," the demon said, "things will have to get messy."

The remaining lights in Enid's house flickered. Outside, thunder boomed. Ember was still unconscious, while Enid dodged the occasional stray energy bolt or spark shower. Her litany of exclamations echoed from where she huddled behind the island in her kitchen—*Oh my! Look out! Get it, Issy!*

The demon attacked, knocking Issy to the floor and straddling her hips. She lay still for a second, stunned, as it reached up onto the table for a slice of pizza.

Strength lagging, Issy closed her eyes and searched for a plan to defeat this demon. *Her talisman.* If she could just get to her purse, maybe she could use it to absorb the electricity the demon was using to zap her energy.

She took a deep breath and heaved with all her might. The slice of pizza went flying as the demon lost its balance and Issy flipped on top.

"Oh, no, you don't!" it screeched, pulling a plug from the wall and aiming it in Issy's face. But Issy was faster. She grabbed a mirror off the wall just in time, directing the energy right back at the demon.

"Ouch!" Its hands flew to its face, and Issy took her chance. She lunged for her purse, grabbing the obsidian talisman and holding it up in front of her.

The demon gasped and shrunk back. She had it! Now, all she had to do was banish it back to Hades, and this would all be over.

Except when she gazed down into the demon's eyes, she saw Raine, not a murderous hell spawn. Removing the demon could harm or even kill her cousin. There had to be another way.

Issy's mind raced for some sort of incantation or special vanquishing spell that would get rid of the demon but leave the host unharmed. But before she could think of it, Enid's front door burst open.

All heads jerked around toward the doorway, where Dex Nolan stood, a confused look on his face. His wide eyes jerked from the burn marks on the wall to the toppled furniture to Issy.

But it was too late. The distraction was all the demon needed to flip Issy to the ground and take control.

Chapter Twenty-Two

"Got you now!" The demon gripped Issy's shoulder tightly in its clawlike hold, and the talisman fell out of her hand. The demon jerked her up off the floor like a rag doll and zipped away with her to the other side of the living room, the room nothing but a blur given the demon's speed.

Issy swayed on her feet, feeling woozy and dazed. An odd force field of some kind glimmered around her upper body. She held her hands in front of her and frowned. An electrical field. The demon had encased her in energy, trapping her magic inside.

Dex rushed to her side, his expression concerned. He reached out, but before she could warn him not to touch her, he got zapped. The demon roared with laughter then mumbled a quick curse. Dex collapsed to the floor, flopping around like a fish as the energy sting ran through him, short-circuiting his muscles.

"That's not fair!" Enid emerged from the kitchen, her tone angry. "He's human!"

"You think I care?" the demon shouted. "I figured all you paranormals would want me to get rid of the FBPI agent in your midst. Maybe you don't care, though, old woman, since you'll be in jail and these others will be dead. Three more homicides on your hands, crone."

The demon raised its arms, its eyes rolling back in its head. Issy wasn't sure what it was doing, but she got the distinct impression it was summoning more energy to finish them all off.

Issy closed her eyes and gathered her inner magic, focusing on breaking the energy bonds the demon had placed around her.

"Liberatium!"

The energy field around her upper body wavered then flickered out.

"Dex!" She squatted down beside Dex, who was shaking off the effects of the energy. He pushed to his feet, shoving Issy behind him and pulling his gun from the holster at his waist. "Stay behind me. I'll take care of this."

"Your bullets won't work here. Not against *that*," she said, pointing toward the demon, who was now rubbing its hands together, creating an enormous arc of sparking energy. "Get down!"

She pushed in front of him, fists curled in a ball, ready to toss out a shield spell to try to ward off at least some of the energy.

"Move aside. I'm not going to screw this one up too." Dex elbowed her out of the way.

"You can't just shoot a demon. You don't know what you are doing!" Not to mention that said demon was in Raine's body. Issy knew for sure a bullet would kill her cousin, and the demon would probably just jump into someone else. She grabbed Dex's arm and tried to wrestle the gun away.

Unfortunately, their argument had bought the demon enough time to gather itself to full strength. A loud crackling came from deep inside the demon as it unleashed a stream of dark-brown negative energy straight toward Dex.

"No!" That much energy would mean certain death for a human. Maybe for a witch too. There was only one thing that she could do to protect him. It might drain all of her energy and leave her defenseless and vulnerable for the demon's next attack—or worse, result in full energy depletion and kill her—but she had no other choice. If she had to give her life to protect Dex, then she would.

She sucked in a breath and curled her fists.

"Praedisium!" She jumped in front of Dex, throwing open her fists and releasing positive energy to form a protective shield that she hoped would stop the negative energy stream.

The air in front of her sizzled, and the smell of burning rubber filled her nostrils. The shield flashed white and then turned into thousands of tiny sparks that rained down at her feet.

It was as if a Mack truck had hit her. The negative energy, now a sickly beige thanks to the lessening effects of the shield, rolled through her body like a tidal wave, throwing her to the floor and sapping her strength before fizzling out into a pile of ash on the carpet.

Issy felt the last drop of energy drain out of her, but with a smug feeling of satisfaction, she noticed the demon had been depleted of energy too. Now if she could just revive hers... But it was too late. She'd drained it down too far, and she was fading fast.

"What the heck?" Dex's voice jerked Issy back awake, and she looked up at him. Their eyes locked just as the demon sent one last lethal surge of energy straight at Issy's heart.

Chapter Twenty-Three

"Issy!" Dex stomped out the smoldering carpet then fell to his knees beside her. What the heck had just happened? His heart raced as he looked at her. Her face was pale, and she appeared to be lifeless. He checked her pulse. Thank God she had one! "Issy, talk to me!"

But she didn't move. He checked her for bleeding. That lightning-bolt thing had hit her in the chest, but the wound was cauterized shut. She wasn't losing blood, thankfully. His world narrowed to Issy, and he forgot about the strange things that were going on and the weird way Raine was acting. The only thing that mattered was Issy. He grabbed her hand.

Please don't die.

Her eyes fluttered and opened for a second, and inside them he thought he saw his whole future before they drifted closed again.

A cackle sounded from the other side of the room, and he jerked his attention to Raine... or the thing that looked like Raine.

"You shouldn't mess in matters of paranormals, human!"

Paranormals? Right. There was no other way to explain this. A million thoughts ran through his head. Stan. Area 59. But the most important one was to protect Issy from that thing. Too bad he'd already bungled that and now she was dying right before his eyes.

He shouldn't have been surprised. He couldn't protect a kidnapped child, and now he couldn't protect Issy. He was a complete and utter failure.

Chapter Twenty-Four

Issy's chest burned as though she'd been poked with a flaming stick. But that was good. Pain meant she was still alive.

She could hear a voice. Dex? The thought comforted her. If he was talking, that meant the demon energy hadn't killed him.

But then another thought jolted her awareness even higher. If she was unconscious, who was going to battle the demon?

She struggled to break through to consciousness like a diver coming up from the depths of the sea, becoming more and more aware of the physical plane as she surfaced. Someone was rubbing her hand, and it felt warm and comforting.

Then she heard a grating noise that churned her stomach. The demon was amping up its power again. Her eyes shot open.

"Are you okay?" Dex was looking down at her, concern etched on his handsome face.

"Yes. You?" Issy tried to sit up, but she was still too weak.

"Yeah, but…"

The demon made another noise, and they both looked in that direction. Dex pulled his gun.

Issy shot her hand out to stop him. Her arm felt as if it were weighted with lead. "No, that won't work."

"What? What the hell is going on here anyway? What is *wrong* with your cousin?"

"She's a demon." Enid spoke from where she was hiding behind the doorway to the kitchen.

"What?" Dex's gaze flicked from Enid to Issy. Issy's stomach sank at the look of disbelief on his face. It was clear Dex didn't believe in demons, even though the evidence was right in front of him, and if he didn't believe in demons when one was shooting energy at him, he sure as heck wasn't going to believe in witches.

The air crackled with electricity, and Raine laughed, rubbing her hands together. "Looks like you are down for the count, Issy. That's too bad. Ember too. Enid's too old to fight me, and now I have all the time I need to get rid of you folks."

"I am *not* too old!" Enid yelled. "Why, I never…"

"The talisman!" Issy tried to push to a sitting position but to no avail. She pointed toward the obsidian talisman that lay under Enid's mahogany end table.

"That egg?" Dex looked perplexed.

Dex stared at it, and Issy's hopes fell. He wasn't going to pick it up. She took a deep breath and summoned all her reserves, hoping she had one last surge in her.

Raine opened her palms, sucked in a breath, and blew a stream of ugly energy toward them.

Issy rolled to the right, grabbed the talisman, and came up on her knees, holding it directly in front of the energy stream.

It hit her with a jolt of electricity. Pain seared up her left arm from the volts, and soon her arm fell limp at her side, and the talisman clattered to the floor, useless. Worse, the deflected energy bounced around the room like a wonky pinball machine, leaving bowling-ball-sized holes in everything it struck—furniture, walls, ceiling, floors.

"Look out!" she managed to call to Enid.

The older woman cowered just in time to avoid a direct hit.

The bouncing energy ball whizzed past Becky, grazing the little pig's side, and she squealed in pain.

"That is enough!" Enid yelled. She stomped into the living room, fury radiating off her petite form in waves. "Bad enough what you've done to my friends and my house. But you will not hurt defenseless animals, do you hear me?" Enid's normally placid face was mottled with rage. "Why, I ought to—"

"Send it back, Enid!" Issy yelled. "You summoned it that day in the alley. Maybe you can send it back!"

"Darn right, I can!" Enid twirled her cane before her like a weapon. "Let's see…" She closed her eyes and aimed the cane at the demon. "Fiddle dee dee. Fiddle dee dum. Get ye back from whence you come!"

BOOM!

There was an explosion of sparks and smoke, and the acrid stench of sulphur clogged the air. Issy held her breath, while Dex covered his eyes and coughed.

Please let Enid's spell work this time. Please let Enid's spell work this time.

Issy repeated the mantra over and over in her head as she peered through the haze to see Raine fall to the floor, limp and soot covered but still breathing. Her complexion had cleared, and the bumps and scratches on her arms had stopped oozing. The demon was gone.

Enid came over to Issy and grinned. "Guess I still got it, eh?"

Chapter Twenty-Five

Issy struggled back onto her knees, surprised that she had the energy even for that. The talisman must have absorbed or deflected almost all of the negative energy, and she was feeling stronger by the second.

"What the heck just happened?" Dex asked. He staggered slightly, his gun waving about as he hacked and coughed. "Issy?"

"Yep. Still down here." She took his hand to help her get to her feet. Her left arm throbbed with pain, but she was more concerned about him. Demons were forbidden from attacking humans for a reason. One bolt of energy could be lethal to their fragile systems. "I'll be fine. What about you?"

"I'm good." He rubbed his watering eyes then squinted around the room. "Like I said, I can take care of myself."

"So can I," she said.

"Yeah." Dex gave her a slow head-to-toe appraisal. "I can see that."

Issy gazed around at the damage. Poor Enid. Her quaint little cottage was trashed. All the small appliances in the kitchen were sputtering and smoking, including the coffee maker and the toaster, not to mention all the lamps. Gaping, charred holes dotted the room from where the energy ball had bounced, and at least half the couch was smoldering. On the dining table, the charcoal-black remains of the poisoned pizza still popped and hissed.

Ember moaned, and Issy rushed to her side. "Are you okay?"

"It's Raine..." Ember managed to whisper. "She's..."

"We know." Issy smoothed the damp auburn hair back from her cousin's forehead and smiled. "Enid banished the demon back to hell."

"She did?" Ember sat up slowly and looked around, pressing her hand to her forehead. "Good for you, Enid."

"Thanks." Enid joined them, and together the trio helped Ember to her feet. "Better check on your third musketeer over there, though."

The Quinn cousins rushed to Raine's side, where she was slumped against the wall. Her eyes fluttered open, and Issy looked deep into them just to make sure. Yep, peridot green and no sign of the deep, dark, fathomless demon

216

soul. Raine wrinkled her nose and scowled up at the other two. "What's going on? What happened? And what's that smell?"

Issy put her arm around Raine's shoulders. "You were possessed by the demon, sweetie. Don't you remember?"

"No." Raine frowned. "The last thing I remember was sitting around Enid's table when we brought over those chocolates. Then I woke up here."

Issy and Ember exchanged a glance. Raine had no idea of the havoc she'd wreaked. How much should they tell her?

"What?" Raine looked around the room. "Are you guys serious?"

"I'm afraid so," Issy said. "Remember how you had those scratches from the briarwort?"

Raine looked at her arms, where the scratches were quickly starting to heal, and nodded.

"That's how the demon got in. My potion in the chocolates did work... Well, sort of. It didn't vanquish the demon. It jumped into you instead because you were weakened by the hives and scratches."

"Did I do all this?" Raine gestured to the room, and Issy's heart twisted at the anguished look on her cousin's face.

"'Fraid so. But that's okay. We'll help Enid clean up, and things will be good as new. No harm done, right, Enid?"

"Of course."

"But I don't remember any of this. What day is it, and what have I been doing since Wednesday?" Raine asked.

"Raine, try to remember that whatever you were doing wasn't actually you. It was the demon. Memory loss is a common side effect of possession, so I'm not surprised you don't remember anything. The same thing happened to Enid that day we brought the chocolates, remember? How do you feel otherwise?" Ember asked.

"I'm a little sore." Raine stretched then winced. "But, otherwise, I'm okay."

"Good." Issy helped her cousin to her feet. "Can I get you some water?"

"No." Raine looked around, her still-shocked expression soon morphing to horror. Tears gathered in her eyes. "Wait a minute. Did I kill someone too?"

"No. You didn't kill anyone." Issy helped Raine into an undamaged dining room chair. "You tried, but the victim survived."

Now it made sense that the victim had heard her assailant arguing. It was Raine, the real

Raine, deep inside the demon, struggling to keep it from killing. Issy felt a rush of pride for her cousin. It must have taken all she had to force her will on the demon from within.

Enid, who stood nearby, clutched the edge of her kitchen cabinets, her face pale. "Did *I*... kill someone?"

"No." Issy rushed to the older woman's side to comfort her. "It wasn't you, Enid. It was the demon who killed that dishwasher."

"Excuse me?" Dex stalked over, his voice razor sharp. "Someone better start explaining all of this to me right now before Owen gets here."

Issy took a deep breath then relayed everything they knew about what happened. The last thing she wanted to do was get Dex involved in their paranormal business, but what choice did she have at that point? It was either tell him the truth, or have him haul Enid, and perhaps Raine, off to prison for crimes they hadn't committed. By the end, at least he didn't deny the paranormal involvement this time. Nor did he threaten any of them with Area 59.

She'd just finished her story when a brief knock sounded on the door, followed by DeeDee and Gray barging in.

"Hey, Quinns. What's going on here?" DeeDee asked.

"Is everything all right?" Gray looked from Issy to Ember to Raine then back again. "I got a text from Raine telling me the meeting here was off and sending me into the boonies instead."

"About that." Issy scrunched her nose. "Turns out Raine was the demon's new host after Enid. Pretty sure it wanted you out of the way. The demon's gone now, though."

"No kidding?" Gray stared wide eyed at Raine. "Are you all right?"

"Yeah, I'm okay." Raine put an arm around Issy and Ember and squeezed them tightly to her sides. "Thanks to these guys. And Enid." Raine shot Enid a grateful glance.

"I'm sorry I didn't get here in time." Gray raked a hand through his uncharacteristically mussed black hair, his aqua eyes sad. "The minute you guys didn't show up at the new location, I knew something was wrong, but then my car died, and I had to call DeeDee to come get me." He glanced over at the deputy and smiled. "Thanks for being my backup."

"I've always got your back, Gray," DeeDee said.

"Thanks." He gave her a friendly nudge on the arm then looked out into the living room and scowled. "What's *he* doing here?"

Issy tracked her cousin's gaze to Dex. "He's here to help."

"Help?" Gray gave Dex a suspicious look. "How? By calling the FBPI on us?"

"I hope not." Issy moved to stand beside Dex, cradling her sore arm. "If he is, then I think I'm the only one they should take. It was me who saw what happened from the beginning, and I didn't report it. The rest of you are innocent bystanders."

She hazarded a glance at Dex, who continued to stare at her with a puzzled expression. He looked as if he was trying hard to remember something. His gaze kept flickering to her lips then back to her eyes as if... Her heartbeat tripled, and she swallowed hard. Did he remember what happened between them in the woods when they caught Christian Vonner?

Shaking his head, Dex finally put his gun away. "I'm not sure exactly what happened here tonight. There's been a lot of crazy electrical phenomena happening in Silver Hollow lately. Summer storms, maybe? I don't know. This place looks a bit trashed, but it doesn't seem to be a police matter. What would you say, Deputy?"

"I agree with your assessment," DeeDee said, shooting Issy a quick wink.

"Good." Dex held Issy's gaze for a few moments more before heading for the door. "From the looks of it, I'd say lightning struck the roof and came out of one of the electrical sockets then ping-ponged around the room. No need to arrest anyone or take anyone in at this time. You might want to call your insurance company, though I'm not sure it's covered. Act of God."

With that, he left.

Issy exhaled slowly, relief washing over her in waves. She wasn't sure if Dex was still in denial about the existence of paranormal activity or if he was generously giving them an out, but either way, he seemed in a hurry to leave her behind. Given the differences between them, Issy couldn't say she blamed him. Honestly, why would an FBPI agent like him want to date a witch?

Her happiness over Raine's and Ember's recoveries floundered slightly, and her chest pinched. She'd liked Dex, and the kiss they'd shared on the boardwalk had been unbelievable, but she wasn't under any illusions. A real relationship between them was doomed. Never mind his job—relationships between humans and witches were notoriously tricky.

Besides, what was important now was that her family was okay and the demon was gone.

Ember frowned at the door then at Issy. "I was awake for the last part of that. You jumped in front of him to save him from the demon's energy. You know what that means."

Sighing, Issy turned away. "It means nothing."

"No." Raine came up beside Ember. "She's right. It means you're responsible for him now. You have a bond."

"Don't be silly. That's just an old wives' tale. It doesn't mean anything." Issy crossed her arms against the sudden chill invading her body. Legend said that if a witch put her life in jeopardy to save a human, that sacrifice created a soul-bond between them. Good thing she didn't put much stock in those old stories.

Otherwise, she might just think there really was something happening between her and Dex, and that would be bad. Bad because he was human and wouldn't be held to the bond the same way she would as a paranormal. He could be free to go off and find his happiness elsewhere while she pined away at home alone for a man who might not ever care for her as much as she did him. She had enough trouble with her love life. No need to add magical twists and soul-bonds to the mix.

"Well, I, for one, am glad we're all okay," Enid said. "That's the important thing."

"Exactly." Issy narrowed her gaze on Raine's arms. "There's barely any sign of those scratches now."

Raine smiled and cocked her chin toward Issy's left arm. "How about you? How are you feeling?" Raine's face fell as she added, "Sorry to cause you any pain."

Issy tested her range of motion. Still achy but not nearly as bad as before. "No worries. It wasn't you, and anyway, I'll live." Then she bent down and held out her hand. "And how's poor little Becky?"

The potbellied pig snorted and trotted over to her for a scratch behind the ears, apparently none the worse for wear.

Enid gave a surprised laugh. "I still can't quite believe that spell worked. You know, I think perhaps all those juice drinks from The Main Squeeze really are helping." She turned toward the table and the still-smoking blackened pizza. "I don't know about you all, but I'm starving. Let me just cast a little un-charring spell on this, and—"

Gray rushed over and pulled Enid into an impromptu hug, lowering her arms to her sides before she could unleash any more wonky incantations. "I'm just so glad you're okay, Enid," he said, giving Issy a "help me here" look over the top of the older lady's head. "I'll take care of dinner, Enid. You must be tired."

"I'm glad you're okay too, young man," Enid said, her voice muffled against Gray's muscled chest. With her short stature, her nose barely reached his upper abdomen. "And I am a bit pooped."

Issy wasn't sure if it was the adrenaline still zinging through her system or the fact that they'd banished the demon and all lived to tell the tale, but the whole situation struck her as funny. Her giggles soon turned into full-blown laughter, and before she knew it, the rest of the family joined in. Even DeeDee, who was watching them all from the side of the room and doing her best to look official, snickered.

Gray finally released Enid, and they all started cleaning up the aftermath of the fight.

"So, that's it, then? We can all go about our business as usual?" Enid said after tossing the remains of the pizza in the trash.

"Not quite, I'm afraid." DeeDee righted a floor lamp. "There's still the matter of Owen. He's looking for a serial killer."

Enid straightened the cushions on the non-scorched half of her sofa then raised her hand. "That would be me."

"You're no killer, Enid Pettywood." DeeDee set an end table back into position beside a toppled chair then crossed her arms. "It was the demon."

"I know, but it was still my body that thing inhabited while it did the awful deed." She stared at her hands, her expression quickly shifting from sadness to horror. "What if there's physical evidence?"

"The only evidence found at the scene of the murder was that charm, the doll, and the meat cleaver," DeeDee said. "Seems the force of the meat cleaver makes you being the killer implausible. Maybe we can just tell Owen you lost the charm?"

Enid fingered the gold bracelet that encircled her wrist. "Is that where that charm went?" She shuddered and held her wrist away from her as if repulsed by the entire bracelet.

"Then we'd have to come up with a whole reason why the killer would have had it. And if Owen doesn't buy that and starts looking into

Enid's whereabouts that day, it won't be good." Issy walked over and put her arm around Enid's quivering shoulders. "We can't let that happen."

"I think I might have an idea of how we can stop it." Gray placed a few knickknacks and doilies back on Enid's shelves then faced the group. "I don't want to say anything specific yet, because I'm not sure it will work. But I'm on it."

Issy rolled her eyes at her cousin's secretiveness. There was definitely something weird going on with him. She hadn't figured out exactly what it was yet, but she would. "Okay, so Gray's handling the whole charm debacle. That still leaves the matter of Luigi. He was gunning for the person who summoned the demon, and I don't think he's going to just forget about it."

"Now there I can help." Enid straightened a bit and raised her chin. "Don't you worry about Luigi Romano. I'll take care of him."

Chapter Twenty-Six

Dex sat in his car in front of Enid's cottage for quite some time, watching the shadows of the people inside through the curtains and just generally doubting himself and his ability to protect anyone. His head was still swimming with everything that had gone down inside, and he hadn't quite sorted it all out yet, but one thing was certain.

As he watched a charcoal-colored cat pace back and forth on the front steps of the house, every so often it would turn its golden-orange gaze on him, and a strange feeling would come over him. A feeling that he was right where he belonged. But that couldn't be true—he didn't belong here, and he certainly didn't belong with Issy.

He hadn't protected her from whatever that thing was in there.

If he closed his eyes, he could still hear its infernal snarls, could still smell the acrid stench of sulphur and taste the tang of fear in his mouth. A lesser man might've sunk to his knees and become a believer in magic. But how else could one explain what had happened?

After a deep sigh, Dex shifted the car into drive and took off slowly down the quiet residential street.

He had to admit, the idea of something beyond our reality existing did intrigue him. Not enough to go around hauling in these so-called paranormals like his partner Stan and subject them to the ghastly experiments he'd heard took place inside Area 59. The thought of that turned his stomach. Instead, when he thought of the people in Silver Hollow having paranormal abilities, he felt protective of them.

His phone rang, and he looked down. It was Stan. The guy had an uncanny ability to call whenever Dex was thinking about him. Maybe he was psychic.

"Nolan here." Dex figured he might as well answer. Otherwise, Stan would keep calling every ten minutes.

Stan's voice was rushed with excitement. "I've got a tip on the underground line something is going down in Silver Hollow right now."

"Oh, that. Yeah. It's nothing. Another issue with the transformer. They have major infrastructure problems here," Dex said.

"Are you sure? My contact said there was weird thunder and lightning but no storm. That's not normal."

"Yep. I checked that all out. I'm tapped in here now to the goings on. You don't have to keep calling. I'm on it."

There was a pause, and then Stan said, "Good. For a while there, I was worried about you."

"Oh?"

"Yeah. You didn't seem like you were exactly on board."

"Oh, I'm on board. I'm keeping a close eye on the residents, and believe me, you will be the first to know if something out of the ordinary happens here."

"Good. Glad to know I can count on you. Keep me posted."

"Will do." Dex hung up, feeling satisfied that he had saved Silver Hollow a visit from Stan. But, at the same time, something twisted in his heart. He'd lied about the job again. Now why had he done that?

As he drove through Silver Hollow, his new home, he started to get that same old feeling in the pit of his gut. The one he'd had for months after that botched kidnapping case at the FBI.

The one that said he was nothing but a big, fat failure.

Dejected, he stopped at a red light near the town green and scowled at his dashboard. Maybe moving here had been a mistake. Honestly, a big part of the reason he'd come back to Silver Hollow had been Issy. And after their date, he'd thought perhaps they had a shot. But now?

Well, after tonight, no way would she want him now. Having the woman you care for and are trying to impress basically throw herself in front of you to shield you from a lightning attack—or whatever those energy ray things were—wasn't exactly the stuff of heroes. And even before that...

He shook his head. Hell, he hadn't even been able to track her on those back roads on the way to the woods. Didn't matter she'd lived here her whole life, that she probably knew all the twists and turns and turnoffs. Tailing a suspect was FBI Training 101.

Man, he was losing it. Big time.

The smart thing would be to go back to headquarters, start fresh all over again.

Only problem was, he couldn't leave. He'd signed a six-month lease on his home and had a six-month contract with the FBPI to handle this area. So he was stuck.

Dex continued on through town and turned again onto the street where he now lived. Tall oak trees lined both sides of the street, and warm light shone out of the windows of the houses he passed by. He started to feel a smidge better. Okay, so maybe he wasn't perfect. Maybe he had screwed up back there at Enid's house. But maybe, just maybe, Silver Hollow could grow to be his new home after all. It was nice here, and the people were friendly enough. There were lots of kids and animals, and the place had a quaint charm many bigger cities had lost along the way. So, yeah. Perhaps staying here wouldn't be such a chore after all.

He'd do his job and keep an eye out to prevent any bad things from happening to this town's good people. Along the way, if he noticed any more of these paranormal happenings, he'd be sure to keep it on the down-low until he was sure. Wouldn't make sense to get the FBPI involved when it was something he could handle himself, right?

Dex pulled into his driveway and smiled.

Yep. He vowed then and there to do his best to keep the townspeople of Silver Hollow safe and secure. Now, if he could just keep his distance from Issy Quinn, that should be a piece of cake.

Chapter Twenty-Seven

Two days later...

Issy sat at the same table at The Main Squeeze where she'd cast that spell to find Enid's charm. Except, this time, all of her cousins were there, along with their familiars and Enid and Becky.

Her left arm only had a slight ache now when she moved it, and Raine's scratches had all but disappeared. Even Mortimer had perked up—his flytrap leaves stretching toward the midday sun as if in worship, the tiny hairs quivering as he awaited some poor unsuspecting insect that he could snap into his clutches. Still, it was good to see he was interested in eating. Poor thing had wilted a lot during Raine's demon possession.

In hindsight, Issy could've smacked herself for missing such an obvious clue. Then again, it wasn't every day a gal's cousin got possessed by a demon.

Bella glanced at Mortimer then up at her, and Issy's heart swelled with pride. When Raine had asked Issy to take care of Morty that night in her house, Bella had acted strangely. Issy had assumed it had something to do with the Venus flytrap's wilting state, but now she realized that Raine had already been possessed by the demon then, and Bella had been growling at *Raine*, trying to warn Issy that something was wrong. Issy hadn't been giving the little pup enough credit. She made a mental note to pay better attention to Bella's attempts at communication. The little dog's instincts were good, even though she did seem to be overly fond of Dex.

Her heart twisted at the memories of their date, the second kiss they'd shared on the boardwalk, how sweet and kind he'd been to her. Then she'd gone and screwed everything up at Enid's, and he'd walked out without saying good-bye. Issy hadn't seen him since. For all she knew, he'd packed up and left town again. Maybe that was for the best, though, since the incident at Enid's had proved to her that things between them could never work out.

Dex's story about a freak lightning storm causing the damage had worked with Owen. Too bad Issy was afraid Dex might have believed it himself because he was in denial about what really happened. It was obvious that Dex would never accept magic, and she was what she was.

236

Not that she would change that—not even for him.

Of course, there was the little problem of them being soul-bonded now, but that was an old wives' tale, wasn't it?

They were all just sitting around, enjoying the peace and relaxation of a warm summer Sunday, when Luigi Romano came around the corner, brandishing yet another pizza box.

Leary after what had happened at Enid's, Issy straightened and held Bella back from sniffing the box too closely. "Having lunch?" she asked, forcing a smile.

"No," Luigi said, flipping the box open. "Try my new recipe."

Issy glanced over at Enid, who smiled encouragingly. "I gave him some help."

Each of the Quinn cousins took a slice, and Issy did have to admit it looked really good. The melty cheese mixed with the spice of the peppers and the rich flavor of sausage and roasted mushrooms. Plus, the sauce held just a hint of sweetness, and the crust all but melted in your mouth. They'd soon devoured the whole pizza.

"So no big fallout with the committee over this, Luigi?" Raine asked tentatively.

"You guys got off lucky. I managed to smooth things over, and Enid won a lot of points because she was the one who sent the demon back. Proved it was unintentional." Luigi nodded at Enid. "You managed to contain the demon in short order. That went in your favor. And, well, let's just say I pulled in a few favors of my own, though I have to say I'm not exactly the committee's favorite field agent." Luigi frowned.

"Really? Did you do something wrong?" Issy remembered him alluding to the fact that he wasn't in their good graces earlier, but with a rogue demon on the loose, she hadn't had time to delve into it. The thought of Luigi being on the outs with the committee somehow made Issy feel better. Maybe she didn't need to always be worrying about him watching what she was doing, after all, if he wasn't a big committee go-by-the-books man.

"Let's say I'm a little unconventional." Luigi brushed pizza crust crumbs from his long beard.

"So they sent you here as punishment?" Ember asked.

Luigi bristled. "No. I mean, not really. It's just that the job here isn't the most exciting, so none of the top wizards wanted to come.

Nothing much ever happens here. Unless the rumblings I hear are true..."

"Rumblings?" Gray asked.

Luigi shrugged. "Some kind of magic feud. A disruption in the balance. Thought it might be you guys and those Southies. Especially when I saw that Knight girl on this side of town, but I guess all is well. Probably just an unfounded rumor."

"So are you staying?"

"Oh yeah. I'm here for the duration. Not much good anywhere else." His eyes turned sad for a split second, then his attention snapped back to the table and his empty pizza carton. "But, hopefully, I won't have to take any drastic action as long as you people keep things on an even keel."

"We'll do our best," Gray said.

"Good, then. Did you like the pizza?"

"Yes."

"Delish."

"Best one I've ever had."

Brimming with pride, Luigi took the empty box to the trash then excused himself to head back to his kitchen.

They waited until he was gone, and Issy turned to Enid. "So you didn't get into trouble? No witch house arrest or familiar lockdown?"

Enid winked. "Not even a slap on the wrist."

"Really?" Issy grinned. "How'd you manage to get back in his good graces?"

"Well, I told him he knew better than to suspect I summoned that demon on purpose." Enid squared her shoulders. "My spells were off, that's all. I'm feeling much better now, thanks to these juices." She held her Turquoise Special high in a toast to the Quinns, her eyes twinkling. "And, besides, where else is Luigi going to get the special mushrooms for my pizza sauce recipe? Only witches can see the mushroom field, not warlocks. I'm his only source. And, honestly, he's not such a bad guy. He overdoes it a bit with the doom and gloom, but he'll come around."

"One problem solved, then, I guess." Issy sat back and sipped her own Pineapple Express before glancing up to see DeeDee approaching. "Howdy, Deputy."

"Hi, Quinns." DeeDee pulled up a chair to their table and took a seat between Issy and Gray. She was dressed in a cute sundress today instead of her normal police uniform. "How's everyone on this gorgeous day?"

"Good," Issy said. "We were remarking on how quickly Enid has managed to patch things up with Luigi so there'll be no repercussions from the committee."

"Yeah. Now, if we could take care of Owen and the murder investigation just as fast, we'd be all set." Raine took a sip of her bright-orange Sunrise Delight. She seemed normal now, but Issy thought she detected something forced about her demeanor. As if she was feigning happiness. Truth was, the past two days, she'd been somewhat guarded and reserved. Not her usual self. Though Issy imagined that was to be expected from one who had recently been possessed by a demon.

"Not a problem." DeeDee leaned back in her chair and slipped on a pair of sunglasses. "Starla Knight talked to him this morning. Told him she'd tracked down the other person she'd sold that same charm to, and it turns out that person is wanted for murder in two other states. *And* his modus operandi is to slip a stick-and-straw doll in with the victim."

"Seriously?" Ember sat forward, a tiny kitten in each hand. "That seems awfully convenient."

"Hey." DeeDee shrugged. "Maybe Owen should double check certain things. Funny thing, though, Dex Nolan was there and apparently checked back with the FBI and convinced Owen that there *was* a voodoo serial killer recently caught and it was the tourist Starla sold the charm to."

"Really? There was?" Ember asked.

DeeDee shrugged. "I couldn't find anything about it. Not sure why Dex would lie to Owen unless he was trying to protect a certain witch and her cousins." DeeDee shot Issy a pointed look.

Issy squirmed in her chair. "I doubt he would do that. He is an FBPI agent, after all."

"Yeah, well, then why hasn't he brought anyone in? He was at Enid's that night."

Issy didn't have an answer for that one. Why hadn't he brought any of them in? Was he covering for them?

DeeDee continued. "I think Owen is a little too trusting, but if it gets Enid and Raine off the hook, I'm all for it. It's no harm to anyone since the real killer really is no longer on the loose. Owen was disappointed he couldn't make the arrest, though. I'm just glad we can finally close this case."

"But what about Dex Nolan?" Raine slid a sideways look at Issy. "He saw everything happen. Now he knows about magic."

"Maybe Luigi erased his memories like he did after the Vonner incident," Issy said.

"No." Enid slipped a piece of pizza crust to Becky. "I asked him about that, and he said it was too risky seeing as he'd just erased his memory less than a month ago. So he should remember everything."

"He's probably in denial," Issy said. "You heard him say it was all because of lightning. Can't bring himself to believe in magic, I bet."

Ember touched her arm gently. "I don't think that's it at all. I think he just needs some time to come to terms with it."

"Whatever. As long as he doesn't bring us to Area 59, he can think what he wants."

"You need to give him a chance."

Issy decided to change the subject. She turned to DeeDee. "So, Starla just wandered in to talk to Owen, huh?" Issy glanced over and caught Gray's gaze before he looked away fast. Yep. He'd definitely been behind that. "That's weird, right? For her to come all the way over from the south side entirely of her own accord."

"Uh-hmm. Not entirely of her accord." The voice came from near her feet, and Issy looked down to see Brimstone blinking up at them. "That's right. I haven't just been sitting around doing nothing while you guys have been doing all the work, you know."

"Oh really? Was it you that got Starla to play nice? I thought it was Gray." Ember slid her eyes over to Gray, who simply shrugged.

"I did go and visit her, but she seemed awfully easy to convince," Gray said. "I thought it was just my boyish charm."

"Don't flatter yourself, buddy." Brimstone's voice was low so that the other patrons couldn't hear him. Though many people in the town were paranormal and wouldn't bat an eyelash at a talking cat, the human population would think it was quite strange. "It was all my doing. And I'll have you guys know I had to wine and dine a certain orange tabby female this whole week to get her to telepath those thoughts into Starla's head."

"Well, thank you. Whatever you did worked," Raine said.

Brimstone sat on his haunches and licked his paw, preening behind the ears. "No problem." He glanced at Bella and then at Endora and Bellatrix, who lay curled around each other like a furry yin and yang symbol, snoozing. "Somebody has to take the reins and get things done."

Issy plucked an orange hair from his tail. "I bet it wasn't all hardship, though, was it?"

"A gentleman never kisses and tells." Brimstone flicked his tail and strutted away.

"What about you, Gray?" DeeDee teased. "Was your involvement all business, or is there something you won't tell?"

"For the last time, there's nothing going on. She's a Knight. We're practically enemies."

"Hey, as long as we caught the real guilty party and that demon's gone for good, it's all cool." DeeDee pushed to her feet. "Be right back. I'm going to get one of those yummy Pomegranate Passions."

Issy kissed Bella's head then watched as the wolf shifter made her way up to place her order with Karen. At the counter, Luigi was selling slices of his new pizza to the juice bar's patrons. It seemed as if he'd be sticking around Silver Hollow for a while too. Which, considering he'd given Enid a pass and helped Karen open this shop, wasn't all bad. "I think maybe Luigi Romano isn't so awful after all," Issy said. "We should give him a chance."

Raine and Ember turned around to stare at the huge bearded man before facing Issy once more.

"Okay," Ember said. "I suppose it could be worse."

"Yeah." Raine snorted. "Like falling head over heels for an FBPI agent."

Issy gave her cousin a look from across the table. "I know you're not talking about me."

"Since you're the only one of us Quinns with a love life right now, I guess I am."

"No love life here." Issy ignored the hollow feeling in her chest and turned her thoughts to more practical matters. They'd all gotten off lucky. Perhaps too lucky, if she thought about things too hard.

Now that things were back to normal, she supposed she should focus back on her everyday life. She still had to work on her pet store slogan. At least now there would be no distractions. The demon was gone, Enid and Raine were free women, and all was right with their little Silver Hollow world.

The only question was... how long would it stay that way?

About Leighann Dobbs

USA Today Bestselling author Leighann Dobbs has had a passion for reading since she was old enough to hold a book, but she didn't put pen to paper until much later in life. After a twenty-year career as a software engineer with a few side trips into selling antiques and making jewelry, she realized you can't make a living reading books, so she tried her hand at writing them and discovered she had a passion for that, too! She lives in New Hampshire with her husband, Bruce, their trusty Chihuahua mix, Mojo, and beautiful rescue cat, Kitty.

Find out about her latest books and how to get discounts on them by signing up at:

http://www.leighanndobbs.com/newsletter

If you want to receive a text message alert on your cell phone for new releases, text COZYMYSTERY to 88202 (sorry, this only works for US cell phones!)

Connect with Leighann on Facebook:

https://www.facebook.com/ leighanndobbsbooks

Also By Leighann Dobbs

COZY MYSTERIES

Silver Hollow

Paranormal Cozy Mystery Series

* * *

A Spell of Trouble

Spell Disaster

Blackmoore Sisters

Cozy Mystery Series

* * *

Dead Wrong

Dead & Buried

Dead Tide

Buried Secrets

Deadly Intentions

A Grave Mistake

Spell Found

Mooseamuck Island

Cozy Mystery Series

* * *

A Zen For Murder

A Crabby Killer

A Treacherous Treasure

Mystic Notch

Cat Cozy Mystery Series

* * *

Ghostly Paws

A Spirited Tail

A Mew To A Kill

Paws and Effect

Lexy Baker

Cozy Mystery Series

* * *

Lexy Baker Cozy Mystery Series Boxed Set Vol 1
(Books 1-4)

Or buy the books separately:

Killer Cupcakes

Dying For Danish

Murder, Money and Marzipan

3 Bodies and a Biscotti

Brownies, Bodies & Bad Guys

Bake, Battle & Roll

Wedded Blintz

Scones, Skulls & Scams

Ice Cream Murder

Mummified Meringues

Brutal Brulee (Novella)

No Scone Unturned

————

Witches of Hawthorne Grove Series:

Something Magical (Book 1)

———

Regency Romance

***

The Unexpected Series:

An Unexpected Proposal

Dobbs Fancytales:

Dobbs Fancytales Boxed Set Collection

———

Western Historical Romance

***

Goldwater Creek Mail Order Brides:

Faith

American Mail Order Brides Series:

Chevonne: Bride of Oklahoma

————————

Contemporary Romance

***

Reluctant Romance

———

Sweetrock Cowboy Romance Series:

Some Like It Hot (Book 1)

Too Close For Comfort (Book 2)

————————

CPSIA information can be obtained
at www.ICGtesting.com
Printed in the USA
BVOW04s0227151216
470892BV00018B/378/P